I0663027

Jade for a Lady

KENDELL FOSTER CROSSEN
Writing as
M.E. CHABER

With a Foreword by
KENDRA CROSSEN BURROUGHS

STEEGER BOOKS / **2020**

PUBLISHED BY STEEGER BOOKS
Visit steegerbooks.com for more books like this.

PUBLISHING HISTORY

Hardcover
New York: Holt, Rinehart & Winston, February 1962.
Toronto: Holt, Rinehart & Winston of Canada, 1962.
Roslyn, NY: Detective Book Club #243, Walter J. Black, Inc., July 1962. (With *The Case of the Blonde Bonanza* by Erle Stanley Gardner and *The Cannibal Who Overate* by Hugh Pentecost.)
London: T. V. Boardman (American Bloodhound Mystery #399), December 1962.

Paperback
New York: Paperback Library (63-204), A Milo March Mystery, #1, January 1970. Cover by Robert McGinnis.

ISBN: 978-1-61827-527-1

Milo March is a hard-drinking, womanizing, wisecracking, James-Bondian character. He always comes out on top through a combination of personality, bluff, bravado, luck, skill, experience, and intellect. He is a shrewd judge of human character, a crack shot, and a deeper character than I have found in most of the other spy/thriller novels I've read. But, above all, he is a con-man—and a very good one. It is Milo March himself who makes the series worth reading.

—Don Miller, *The Mystery Nook* fanzine 12

Steeger Books is proud to reissue twenty-three vintage novels and stories by M.E. Chaber, whose Milo March Mysteries deliver mile-a-minute action and breezily readable entertainment for thriller buffs.

Milo is an Insurance Investigator who takes on the tough cases. Organized crime, grand theft, arson, suspicious disappearances, murders, and millions and millions of dollars—whatever it is, Milo is just the man for the job. Or even the only man for it.

During World War II, Milo was assigned to the OSS and later the CIA. Now in the Army Reserves, with the rank of Major, he is recalled for special jobs behind the Iron Curtain. As an agent, he chops necks, trusses men like chickens to steal their uniforms, shoots point blank at secret police—yet shows compassion to an agent from the other side.

Whatever Milo does, he knows how to do it right. When the work is completed, he returns to his favorite things: women, booze, and good food, more or less in that order....

THE MILO MARCH MYSTERIES

Hangman's Harvest
No Grave for March
The Man Inside
As Old as Cain
The Splintered Man
A Lonely Walk
The Gallows Garden
A Hearse of Another Color
So Dead the Rose
Jade for a Lady
Softly in the Night
Uneasy Lies the Dead
Six Who Ran
Wanted: Dead Men
The Day It Rained Diamonds
A Man in the Middle
Wild Midnight Falls
The Flaming Man
Green Grow the Graves
The Bonded Dead
Born to Be Hanged
Death to the Brides
The Twisted Trap: Six Milo March Stories

This is for Lisa—and I wish that each page were a bit of *ke yu.*

CONTENTS

FOREWORD

The Chinese Connection

Jade for a Lady (1962) was the tenth Milo March novel, but appeared as the first novel in the Paperback Library series published in the early 1970s. It is the first of three books in which Milo goes to Hong Kong.

The publisher of Paperback Library chose not to issue the books in chronological order, which could sometimes be confusing for fans, since there were often continuous story lines and returning characters. As a publishing professional myself, I assume they arranged the books in a sequence they considered appealing, starting the series with a strong book. I'm guessing they published *Jade for a Lady* first not just because of the fast-paced action and exotic atmosphere, but because of the lady in the title.

The lady in the title is Mei Hsu, who is Milo's favorite of the many women in his life—from one-night stands to relationships that last for the duration of a case. Mei is the only woman he returns to, and who returns to him. The daughter of a wealthy river pirate, she is a real lady: tall and attractive, feminine, Western-educated (at the elite Smith College), and independent—and she and Milo make beautiful music together. After her father's death, Mei runs his illegal business, earning the sobriquet of Dragon Lady of Hong Kong. Her gang of men steals national treasures from the mainland, to preserve them or to turn the proceeds over to refugees from Communist China.

Although Milo makes his first trip to Hong Kong in *Jade for a Lady*, his connection with Chinese culture goes back to his Army days, when he was one of the first men sent in to help drive the Japanese out of China. He learned fluent Mandarin and Cantonese and apparently came to appreciate the ancient Chinese poets. The quoting of Oriental wisdom sayings in the Milo March series is a holdover from the pulps that Ken Crossen wrote under the pen name Richard Foster, including the fourteen Green Lama stories (1940–1943), *The Laughing Buddha Murders* (1944), and *The Invisible Man Murders* (1945). Milo is also well versed in Chinese etiquette, almost to the point of parody, and patiently exchanges humilities with old man Hsu. "Most of our conversation was over which one of us was being honored," he says later, yet he seems to genuinely enjoy it.

Milo's other pleasures—food and drink, not necessarily in that order—are also fulfilled in Hong Kong, including Peking duck, shrimp with garlic, steak and sour vegetables, bean curds in oyster sauce, strong Chinese wine, and Lor Mai Tsao whiskey.

Mei Hsu makes further appearances when Milo returns to Hong Kong in *A Man in the Middle* (1967) and *Green Grow the Graves* (1970). In the last novel published in Ken Crossen's lifetime, *Born to Be Hanged* (1973), Mei flies to America to meet Milo where he is on the job in Reno, Nevada, thus relieving an otherwise tough story with

ILLUSTRATION BY ROBERT MCGINNIS

a mostly male cast. They also discuss marriage. That is, Mei asks Milo why he doesn't marry her. Milo regretfully explains that he wouldn't be able to accept being "Mr. Hsu." And, frankly, Milo's lifestyle wouldn't be fair to Mei. But it is a model relationship while it occurs. As Milo later acknowledges, "I was more fond of her than I usually cared to admit."

Mei Hsu is portrayed on two of the spectacular Robert McGinnis covers in the Paperback Library series: bikini-clad in number 1 (number 10 in this series) and topless in number 19 (in both series).

Kendra Crossen Burroughs

ONE

The name is March. Milo March. I'm an insurance investigator. For one hundred dollars a day and expenses. Some people think this ought to make me rich. Maybe it would, if I worked every day in the year. But there are long dry spells when all I do is sit around in my office and wait. ...

The phone rang. I picked up the receiver and said hello. "Mr. March," a strange voice said, "this is Robert Carlin, manager of the Claims Bureau of the Personal and Inland Marine Insurance Association."

"Yes?" I said. It didn't mean much to me. I'd heard of the Association, but that was all.

"Your name was suggested to me by Martin Raymond of Intercontinental Insurance," he said. "Intercontinental is one of our member companies. I wonder if you might come down and talk to me?"

"I guess it could be managed," I said casually. "What do you have in mind?"

"I'd rather talk about it when we meet. Can you make it today? For lunch?"

"I don't see why not."

"Twelve?"

"I'll be there," I said.

"Good," he said, and hung up.

I replaced the receiver and opened the phone book. I looked up the Association. They were way downtown on John Street. I picked up the phone and dialed the number of Intercontinental. When they answered, I asked for Martin Raymond. I repeated the request and added my name when his secretary answered.

"Milo," he said, coming on. "How's the boy?"

"Still a boy," I said, "if you're careless with a few years. I just had a call from Robert Carlin. What's the bit?"

"I don't know," he said. "Carlin is head of Claims for the Association. We had lunch the other day, and he mentioned that they were thinking of hiring an outside man for a special job. I suggested you. That's the whole script."

"What's the job?"

"He didn't tell me."

"What kind of a man is Carlin?" I asked.

"Top drawer. He's a former FBI man and has been with the Association for about fifteen years. We're a member, but we've never asked them to do an investigation for us. I'm told that they do a hell of a good job when they're called in."

"Well, thanks for the plug—I think."

"Nothing," he said. "You know that I'm always in your corner, boy."

"It's nice having you in my corner," I said, "except for the times when you have your thumb in my eye."

He chuckled, but it was an executive type sound without any meat on it. "That's my boy. Always making with the old laugh meter. Well, I'll see you around, boy."

"I suppose so," I muttered, putting the phone down. I looked at my watch. It was shortly after ten-thirty.

There wasn't much chance that I'd get another phone call. Most of my business came from Intercontinental. I called my answering service and told them I'd be back by two or two-thirty. I went downstairs and went to the nearest bar for a martini. By the time I'd finished it, it was time to go. I got a cab and told the driver to take me to John Street.

It's a funny thing. I've traveled all over the world on jobs, but when I'm in New York, anything that isn't Greenwich Village, where I live, or Madison Avenue in the mid-forties, where my office is, seems like a major safari. In fact, I'd never been to John Street.

It turned out to be a narrow, busy street. The taxi deposited me in front of number 60 and I went in. A glance at the board in the lobby showed me that the building was full of insurance companies. I went up to Personal & Inland Marine and was shown into Carlin's office.

He was a wiry little man, probably about fifty. His office, in size and furniture, was pretty much what I was accustomed to seeing in insurance companies—but he wasn't. He wore a dark shirt and tie and a rumpled suit, which made him look more like an artist than either a vice-president or a former Federal agent. "Let's go to lunch," he said as soon as we had shaken hands.

We went downstairs and walked a couple of blocks to Whyte's. It's a restaurant so old, it's practically a tradition downtown. We got a table upstairs and ordered a couple of drinks.

"Are you free to take a job?" Carlin asked when we had our drinks.

"I guess so," I said. "Depends on what it is. I didn't know you handed out jobs."

"We usually don't. We have six men in the department and they can handle about all we do, but it keeps them busy. That's why I decided to look around for someone to take this case. If I used one of my own men on it, he might be away too long. Martin Raymond said that you were the best man he knew."

"Martin doesn't know very many," I murmured.

He smiled. "I did some other checking on you before I phoned. You may not have the background that my men have, but it strikes me that you're just as good."

"What's the job?" I asked.

"It's really two jobs," he said. "One of our member companies—Great Northern Insurance, to be exact—carried a large policy on a necklace of imperial emerald jade owned by a man here in New York. It was stolen last week. We want you to find it."

"You've at least made me curious," I said. "I know Great Northern. I used to do some work for them. They have a pretty good bunch of their own investigators. And you've got your men. I don't like to be nosy, but how come you're passing up so many good investigators for a guy named March? Just for one little necklace."

"I told you there were two jobs," he said with a smile. "When this necklace was taken, it was the only thing stolen, although it was in a wall safe with other jewelry. It's true that the other pieces weren't as valuable as this one, but they didn't come from the five-and-ten."

"How valuable was the necklace?"

"It was insured for one hundred thousand dollars."

I whistled softly. "It must have been good jade."

"The best. Some of the stones in the necklace were more than two thousand years old."

"Go on," I said. "I still haven't heard anything about the second job."

"In the past five years," he said, "member companies of our association have paid out about two million dollars on stolen jade jewelry. All of it good stuff. We've done a little checking and have discovered that other insurance companies have paid out about four million dollars during the same period on jade that was stolen. In some cases other jewelry was taken with the jade, but most times only the jade was stolen. The other jewelry has all shown up somewhere since, but not a single piece of jade has been seen after it was stolen."

"Somebody's collecting jade?" I asked.

He nodded. "Looks that way. We believe that all of the thefts were committed or engineered by the same person or persons. Since the thefts have occurred all over the world, it must mean a large and well-organized gang. That's the second job. It'll give you an idea of what you'll be up against."

"Only if I get close enough," I said, shrugging. "What about known jewel thieves? Have they been checked out?"

"Pretty thoroughly. We believe that none of them has been involved in this."

"Any files on the other cases?"

"The ones from our member companies. We don't have files on the others. This latest theft, however, may be your best lead, as it's fresher. If you find the necklace, I think you'll be right in the middle of the second job."

"Maybe ..."

"Of course, you can conduct the investigation any way you want to," he said with a smile. "I've already been warned about telling you how to do it."

"Who warned you?"

"Remember John Franklin?"

I nodded. "In charge of investigations for Great Northern. A good man."

"He said the same thing about you. In fact, he was quite pleased when I told him we were considering you for the job. But he told me that I'd better accept the fact that you'd do it your own way."

"It's my way of working," I said bluntly.

"It's all right with me," he said easily. "My information is that you nearly always get results. That's all we're interested in."

"Who would I be working for? You or the other companies involved?"

"For us."

"No interference from the other companies?"

"I guarantee it."

"Do you know my rates?" I asked. "A hundred dollars a day and expenses."

"That is satisfactory. In fact, I think I can promise you that if you pull this off, there will also be a substantial bonus."

"I won't fight it," I said. "I'm very fond of money. Do you have a file on the necklace job?"

"Not much of one. I'll give it to you when we get back to the office. The necklace belonged to Maxwell Halley, who lives up on Park Avenue. He and his wife were out that evening, and it was the servants' night off. The thief broke in by jimmying the lock on one of the rear doors, and opened the wall safe without damaging it. That's about all we know."

"Somebody who knew the combination?"

"That or someone with an electronic device which permitted him to detect the fall of the tumblers."

"I suppose the servants were all checked?"

"Thoroughly. The police are inclined to think they're clean. Mr. Halley swears that none of them knew the combination."

"The wife?"

He grinned at me. "She was one of our first thoughts. And the police's. She's thirty years younger than her husband. But he also swears that she didn't know the combination, and the police couldn't stir up even a breath of scandal about her."

"Okay," I said. "Some of my best friends are cops, but I think I'll check it out myself."

"Good," he said.

We had another drink and then ate lunch. I went back to the office with him, and he gave me the Halley file and a check for a thousand dollars for advance expenses. It looked lovely. I went back uptown to my office.

The file didn't tell me much more than Carlin had. Maxwell Halley was a sixty-year-old industrialist, still active in his business and worth several million dollars. His wife was thirty. She was his second wife, and they had been married five years. He had two grown children by his first wife. The

Halleys owned considerable jewelry, which was usually kept in a bank vault, being taken out only when it was to be worn, and then it might be kept in the apartment wall safe for a day or two. The insurance company and the police had questioned Mr. and Mrs. Halley and their servants, but the result was nothing. They weren't even suspicious of anyone. The police had taken the usual steps, but no trace of the necklace had been found. At the time of the theft there had been other jewelry in the safe, valued at about five thousand dollars, but it had not been touched. There had also been about a hundred dollars in cash. It had been left there.

I picked up the phone and dialed the number of Great Northern. I asked the operator for John Franklin.

"Milo March," I said, when he answered.

"Milo," he exclaimed. "It's a long time since I heard from you. How are you?"

"Fine. And you?"

"Great. I was talking about you with someone the other day."

"I know. I've taken the job."

"I'm glad to hear it, Milo. I told Carlin you were the man for the job."

"Thanks, John," I said. "I've been looking through the file. Not much in it."

"Not much," he admitted.

"The police dig up anything that isn't in the file?"

"Not a thing."

"What about the time since the file was typed up? Anything turn up since then?"

"No."

"You sound too damn cheerful for a man whose company just lost a hundred grand," I said.

"Why not?" he asked. "The brass here may be a little worried because they don't know what good hands we're in. I stopped worrying when Carlin said he was going to hire you."

"Thanks for nothing," I muttered. "All I seem to have been given so far is a headache. Usually there's something to go on. You have any ideas on this?"

"Not really, Milo," he said. "I don't think the necklace was taken by any of the known jewel thieves or by anyone in the Halley household. I'm inclined to go along with Carlin in believing there is a big international outfit of new faces. I doubt if you'll even find them in this country."

"You think the servants are all out?"

"I think so. That's what the cops think, too."

"What about the wife—or one of her friends?"

He chuckled. "Go see them and make up your own mind, Milo. I think you'll agree with us. You're trying to make the job too easy for yourself."

"What does that mean?"

"If it were the wife, or one of her boyfriends, we wouldn't need you. We would have it wrapped up. It's much bigger than that, Milo."

"I don't like big things," I said sourly. "Tell me something, John. Those other robberies that Carlin mentioned—most of the jade that was taken was Chinese, wasn't it?"

"Well, in a way," he said. "At least, at some time or other, it had mostly been Chinese-owned. But I'm told that it didn't originate there, that China got its jade primarily from Burma or Chinese Turkestan. Why do you ask?"

"I just thought of something," I said. "Suppose this big gang you and Carlin keep mentioning turns out to be Red China trying to get all its jade back. What do I do then?"

"If I know you, you'll walk into Red China and bring it back."

"Funny man," I said. "I should know better than to waste my time talking to you about it. See you around, John."

"Good luck, Milo," he said. He was chuckling as he hung up.

I cursed to myself and took another look at the report There was a notation that Halley was usually home by four in the afternoon. I glanced at my watch. It was just three o'clock. That would give me time to go see Mrs. Halley before he arrived. I left.

The Halleys lived in the better section of Park Avenue. A doorman called upstairs to see if I was to be thrown out. He looked disappointed when the answer was obviously no. I went up in the elevator and was met at the door by a maid. She led the way into the living room.

The woman who waited for me there was tall, blonde, and extremely attractive. She wore a dark gown that covered her from her neck to well below her knees, but managed to suggest much that was beneath it. She appeared to be younger than the thirty stated in the report.

"Mr. March?" she asked as I came in. "I believe that you said you represent our insurance company?"

"That's right," I said. "You're Mrs. Halley?"

She nodded. "Won't you sit down? I hope this visit means that you have some news about my necklace."

I took the chair across from her. "I'm afraid not, Mrs. Halley. As a matter of fact, I just started working on the case today. The company is hoping that I will be able to find it. I wanted to ask you a few questions."

"More questions?" she said with a little gesture of annoyance. "But we've already told everything to two different men from the insurance company, as well as to the police."

"I've read their reports," I said, "but it's not quite the same as hearing the information for myself. I hope you won't mind telling it once more. … You and your husband were out the night the necklace was stolen?"

"Yes. At the theater."

"And the servants?"

"They were all out, too. We'd given them the night off."

"The necklace was in the safe?"

"Yes."

"Did you always keep it there?"

"No. We kept it in a safe-deposit box at the bank along with my other jewelry. It was only taken out when I was going to wear it."

"And were you going to wear it that night?"

"No. I had worn it the night before. There had been no opportunity to return it to the bank."

"Wasn't that unusual?"

"No. My jewelry is often left in the apartment safe for three or four days. The safe is quite good."

"But not good enough this time," I commented. "Was the lock on the safe broken?"

"No. Someone managed to open it."

"Perhaps one of the servants?"

"No. My husband says that they did not know the combination. And the police have proved that each of them was where he or she claimed to be that night."

"Was it generally known the necklace was here that night?"

"I don't think so."

"But the servants probably knew it was here?"

"I suppose they might have known it," she said. "But we trust them completely."

"Who knew the combination of the safe?"

"My husband."

"Perhaps it was written down somewhere in case he forgot it?"

"I don't believe so."

"And you didn't know it?"

"No."

"Perhaps you knew it at one time," I said with a smile, "and then forgot it. And you might have mentioned it to a friend without suspecting they might sometime make use of it."

"No," she said firmly.

Before I could ask another question there was a cheery hello from the direction of the hallway, and a moment later a man entered the room where we sat. He was tall and handsome, with gray hair. He looked to be about fifty, although I guessed he was Mr. Halley and knew from the report that he was ten years older.

"This is my husband," she said to me. She stood up and kissed him as he came up to her. "Maxwell, this is Mr. March from the insurance company. About the necklace."

"Have you found it?" he asked.

"No," she said before I could answer. "Mr. March has just been assigned to the case, and he has come to ask the same old questions." She looked up at him and laughed. "I believe Mr. March had just gotten to the point of thinking I stole the necklace myself or gave the combination to my secret lover." Her husband looked at me with laughter in his eyes. "You must forgive us, Mr. March," he said, "but that was the first thing the police thought of. My wife is thirty years younger than I am, and this seems to put all sorts of ideas into people's heads. We find it very amusing."

"Well ... ," I said lamely. I wasn't sure what to say, since I was partly guilty of the same charge.

"I'll tell you the same thing I told the police," he said. "My wife doesn't know the combination to the safe only because there's been no need for her to know it. My wife and I have a joint bank account. Even if she had a lover, she wouldn't have to steal her own jewelry to get money for him. She could merely cash a check. I trust her completely and never ask her what she has done with the money she withdraws. I don't even see her canceled checks."

"Okay," I said. "So I'm paid to have a nasty mind. As a matter of fact, your premiums go to pay me to have a nasty mind. Sometimes it may offend you, but most of the time it works out to your benefit. Tell me something else. Isn't a hundred thousand dollars a lot of money for a necklace like that?"

"Not really," he said. "The necklace is worth much more than that. It consisted of imperial emerald jade, and several of the beads dated from the time of Emperor Ch'ien Lung, in the eighteenth century. There is no other necklace like it in the world."

"Since the thieves took the necklace and nothing else, would you say that they knew the value of what they were getting?"

"Definitely. The other pieces in the safe were more flashy in appearance."

"And you have no idea of who might have engineered the robbery?"

"No."

"Mrs. Halley said that you trust the servants. Have any of them quit or behaved in an unusual manner since the robbery?"

They both looked startled. "Well ... ," she said, then stopped and looked at her husband.

"One of our maids did leave three days ago," he said, "but we are sure there is no connection. She left because her sister was going to have a baby."

"The robbery was eight days ago?"

"Yes."

"What was the maid's name?" I asked.

"Mary Moy."

"Chinese?"

"Yes," he said reluctantly. "But don't jump to conclusions because she's Chinese and the necklace is jade."

"If she's innocent, she won't be hurt by the conclusions I jump to," I said. "Do the police know about her leaving?"

"N-no. They haven't been around since she left. And, as I said, we're sure there is no connection."

"Do you have an address for her?"

"Of course," he said. "I'll get it." He left the room.

"Mrs. Halley," I asked when he was gone, "how long did this girl work for you?"

"About two months." She must have noticed the expression on my face. "Don't try to make something out of that, too. She came very well recommended and she was a wonderful maid."

"I'm sure she was," I said gravely. "What was she like?"

"Young and beautiful. In fact, we were worried at first, because we thought she'd want to be going out on dates all the time. ... Oh yes, and she was quite tall for a Chinese."

"Did you see any of her boyfriends?"

She shook her head. "If she had any, they never came here. And she didn't go out often. She was the best maid we ever had."

Maxwell Halley came back, carrying a small account book. He gave me an address on Pell Street.

"I hope," he concluded, "that you won't be rough with her, Mr. March. She's a fine girl."

"I won't be rough," I said. I stood up. "Thank you very much. I'm sorry that I had to bother you."

They both muttered polite nothings and I left. I took a cab down to Chinatown. I didn't expect to find anything, and I was right. A Mary Moy *had* stayed at the address, or at least had a room there for exactly two months. She'd given it up three days earlier. No one knew where she came from or where she had gone. No one knew anything about her, not even when I asked in Chinese. I wasn't making much headway. I needed some kind of lead, and there was one place I might get it.

I headed back uptown, to Broadway and Vinnie's Sport Palace. It was a place with every kind of game and coin machine you could think of, plus a shooting gallery and all sorts of novelties. The man I wanted to see could usually be found there—if he wanted to be found. I looked around on the street level, but didn't see him. I walked over to the novelty counter.

"Little Pete around?" I asked the man behind the counter.

"Might be," he said. "And again, might not be. Who's looking for him?"

"Tell him Milo March is downstairs practicing to take him on at Skee-ball."

I turned and headed for the stairs without looking back. I went down to the basement and over to the Skee-ball games. You roll a wooden ball up an incline so that it jumps into one of several circles, with the score running from ten to fifty for each ball. There's nothing much to it, but just try to rack up a decent score. I put a coin in the slot and released the balls. I threw the first one. Ten points. I tried another one. Ten points again. I did worse on the third one. Nothing.

"Hiya, Milo," a new voice said. It was Little Pete. "You still ain't throwing them balls the way I told you to. You gotta put the old mazoo on them. Like this."

He picked up three of the balls and threw them one after the other with apparent carelessness. But he scored fifty points with each ball.

"Like that," he said as the third ball plunked into the center circle.

"If there were such a thing," I said, "as a Skee-ball championship, I'm sure you'd hold it, Pete. Want to play a game?"

"For how much a point?" he asked, grinning.

"That depends on what you know."

"Huh?" he said.

"You know anything about a jade necklace theft up on Park Avenue a little over a week ago?"

He looked at me out of the corners of his eyes. "What kind of things?"

"Anything at all. Even a lead to somebody else who might know something."

He squinted at the Skee-ball game. "Seems to me I heard of it," he said. "You want to play?"

"Sure," I said. "I'll bet fifty dollars I can beat you."

"Okay," he said. He made a pretense of searching through his pockets. "You got two dimes? I'm in Flatsville."

I dug two dimes out of my pocket, dropped them in the slots, and released the balls for two games. I picked up a ball and threw it. I scored ten points.

"What do you know?" I asked.

He chose a ball, sighted carefully, and let go. It leaped nimbly into the fifty-point circle. "I heard there's a guy in Chinatown who maybe knows something about that job." He picked up another ball and sighted.

"Who's the guy?"

"Cheung Tai." He let the ball go. Another fifty points.

"Where do I find him?"

He waited until he'd thrown another ball and racked up another fifty points. "There's a restaurant down there by the name of Ling Fat."

"I know it," I said. "I've eaten there many times. It's got good food, but I never saw any stoolies around."

"Maybe you wasn't looking for anything but the chow," he said. He threw another ball, and it followed the path of the first three. "The way I hear it, he hangs out there the way I do here."

"Okay. Who's this Cheung Tai? Did he pull the job?"

"The way I hear it, he just knows something about it."

"Do you know anything about a Mary Moy?"

He thought a minute, then shook his head. "I never heard the name before."

"You know anything else about the job?" I asked.

"You know I don't hold out on you, Milo," he said. "I just happen to hear by accident that this China boy knows something. I don't think it was any of the regulars what pulled the job, or I would hear more."

"Okay," I said. I gave up my own Skee-ball game and watched him while he ran up a perfect score. I took out fifty dollars, gave it to him, and left.

Ling Fat's was a small basement restaurant on one of the winding, narrow streets in Chinatown. It certainly was no tourist trap. Many times when I'd gone there, I'd been the only Westerner in the place. It was that way this time.

One of the waiters recognized me and came over. He said hello in his own language and I answered in it. I asked him how his family was and he assured me that they were fine. I ordered my food. Shrimp with garlic, steak and sour vegetables, and a side order of bean curds in oyster sauce. The waiter started to leave.

"Is Cheung Tai around?" I asked.

He turned and gave me a startled look. *"Shen ma?"* he asked.

"Cheung Tai," I repeated. "I would like him to join me so that we may talk."

"I will see," he muttered, and left.

When he came back several minutes later, he was carrying a bottle of almost white liquid and two bowls. He placed them on the table.

"If you would have Cheung Tai join you," he said, "you must serve him wine. I will put it on your bill."

"Please do," I said, but he was already moving away.

I didn't see him coming. Suddenly there was a small Chinese, with a thin, wrinkled face, standing at my table. He bowed.

"I am Cheung Tai," he said in Chinese. "I am honored that you have invited me to share your food."

I hadn't, but if he wanted to eat and drink, I wasn't going to argue with him. "No, it is I who am honored," I said in the same language. "You will make me happy if you consent to share my poor meal. I am called Milo March."

He bowed again and sat down across from me.

"May I pour you some wine?" I asked.

"I am doubly honored," he said, and waited.

I poured wine into the two bowls and passed one to him. I lifted my own bowl and tasted the wine. It was as powerful as any whiskey.

He drank his wine and was silent for several minutes. Finally he looked at me shrewdly.

"Why does the strange American," he asked, switching to English, "come to the restaurant of Ling Fat to see Cheung Tai?"

"I am told that Cheung Tai is a man who knows many things."

"I have lived a long time," he said, "and if one lives long enough, one learns much."

"Such as what happened to a jade necklace?" I asked. "Many of the beads on the necklace were from the days of the Emperor Ch'ien Lung."

"This information is important to you?" he asked.

I knew a bite when it was being put on me. "How much?" I wanted to know.

He stared at me. "I am an old man, and it is not always easy to get enough rice. Sometimes, too, it is dangerous to know things." He consulted the wine in his bowl. "Fifty dollars."

"I will pay you fifty dollars if you have any information that is worth it."

"How do I know that you will not lie to me about the worth and pay me nothing after I have talked?"

"I will pay if it is worth it."

He sighed heavily. "One must trust even strangers. What is it you would know?"

"Do you know who stole the jade necklace?"

"I was not there," he said carefully. "And no one has come directly to me with the information. But I am a man who observes many things and can place them together in the proper order."

"You think you know who stole the necklace?" I asked.

He nodded. "I do not know his name. He was of my people, but no one here knew him. He came every night for two months and talked to no one. He left as suddenly as he came."

"But you know that he stole the necklace?"

"It was obvious."

"How was it obvious?"

"I remember about the robbery," the old man said. "Because it was imperial jade, it impressed me. And I remember that the night of the robbery this man was excited when he came here. The next morning he was here and reading the newspapers that told of the robbery. It was the first time he had ever read a newspaper here. And he left that same day, never to return."

I groaned to myself. "That is all?"

"But what else is needed?"

"A few facts might help," I said. "All you know is that there was a man here who read the newspaper account of the robbery and then left. That is the whole thing."

"Not all," he said with dignity. He helped himself to more wine. "This one was here for no good. Ask anyone. He came here suddenly and waited, not talking to anyone. He was dressed well and he had plenty of money. And he saw no one but the girl."

"The girl?" I asked. My interest was renewed.

"Yes. Also one of my people. And a stranger. She was young and tall, and as beautiful as the lotus flower. They met here once every week for the two months. But it was not a meeting of lovers. They were always like two merchants meeting to sell fish."

"And I suppose she left the day after the robbery, too?"

"No," he said. "She left five days later."

I was beginning to be interested. The girl and the man had been here for two months. Mary Moy had worked for the Halleys for two months. The girl had left three days ago—the same time that Mary Moy quit working as a maid.

"I suppose no one knows the girl's name either?" I said.

"Aha," he said. He tapped the side of his head. "It is there that you underestimate Cheung Tai. I know the girl's name and where she went when she left here."

The waiter arrived with food. I noticed that he had a separate order for Cheung Tai. He put the dishes down and left.

"Well?" I said, when he was gone.

"It is here," Cheung Tai said, "that we must pause to make the arrangements. I believe there was a mention of fifty dollars." He uncovered one of the dishes and began to serve himself with his chopsticks.

I decided that it was probably a good gamble. I took fifty dollars from my pocket and slid it across the table. He looked at the bill carefully before putting it in his pocket.

"You are a man of honor," he said. "It is not often that I have the pleasure of doing business with such a man."

"Who was the girl?"

"She called herself Mary Moy, but I do not believe that was her real name."

"When did you last see her?"

"Three days ago in this restaurant. It was then that she left."

"For where?"

"Hong Kong."

"How do you know this to be true?"

"When she was last here, she went to use the telephone. The walls of the telephone booth are not thick and I heard the conversation. She was asking about her reservation on an airplane for Hong Kong. It was then that I also learned her name."

"You just happened to be by the phone, I suppose," I said.

"Of course," Cheung Tai answered blandly. "I had marked her and the young man when they first came here. It had occurred to me that there might be a time when information about them could be valuable. You see that I was right."

"Apparently. And when did you last see the man?"

"A week ago, when he met the girl here for the last time. He has not been back since that day."

"What happened between them that day?"

"I could not hear their words, but he gave her a package and she gave him something which I believe was money."

"How large a package?"

"Large enough to contain a jade necklace," he said with a smile.

I began to think I had finally bought something. Everything seemed to fit. I finished my meal and hurried back to my office. I found Carlin's home phone number and called him there. I told him what I'd learned. He agreed that I should follow it up. He told me to make a reservation for Hong Kong and he'd have more expense money for me in the morning. I called Pan American and made the reservation. Then I went downtown.

I stopped in at the Blue Mill, had a drink, and talked for a few minutes with Alcino and Freddie. I went to the liquor store and bought a bottle of V.O. from Martha, then went on to my apartment on Perry Street. There was no mail except for a couple of bills. I walked up the two flights and unlocked my door. I stepped inside.

He was sitting on the couch. He was tall and slim, almost emaciated. He was not old, but his hair was pure white. It was cut very short. His eyes were milky blue, so light they looked like snow in the shadows. There was no expression on his face as he looked up.

There was a gun in his hand. Pointed at me.

TWO

For a minute we stared at each other, neither of us moving. The gun continued to point steadily at me. I reached around and slowly closed the door behind me.

"I hope," I said, "that I didn't inconvenience you by entering without knocking."

"No," he said.

I walked over to my kitchenette and put down the bottle of whiskey. I turned and started to cross the room to my desk in the corner of the living room.

"No," he said.

I stopped. "No what?" I asked.

"I cased the place," he said. "I know you got a gun in the bedroom and another one in the desk. I left them there, but don't try to get one of them."

I shrugged and turned back. "I don't get it," I said. "There must be some mistake."

"You're Milo March?"

There was little point in denying it. I nodded.

"Then there's no mistake."

"So there's no mistake," I said. "What's the score? Whose toes have I been stepping on now?"

"I don't know," he said. "I get my orders and that's all."

"You mean this isn't a warning call?"

He shook his head.

"Then what's the program?"

He glanced at his watch. "In about seven minutes you're going to turn on your television set. One of my favorite Western shows is coming on then, and it has a lot of shooting in the opening." He stared at me with no expression in his face. "Nobody will pay any attention to one more shot."

So that was it. I thought furiously for a minute. I hadn't been on a case in recent weeks until this one. I'd been on this one less than a day, but he still must be linked to it. Maybe somebody had kept an eye on the Chinese restaurant, or maybe Cheung Tai had a second customer.

"Does it have to do with jade?" I asked.

"I don't know. All I know is I have a contract for you."

"Who gave you the contract?"

He shook his head, giving me a flat grin. He glanced at his watch again. That reminded me that I didn't have much time. If I was going to do anything, it had to be soon. "Mind if I have a drink?" I asked.

"No."

"Would you like one?"

"What've you got?"

"Gin and Scotch and some good V.O."

"Scotch and water," he said. "You'd better hurry it up. It's almost time."

I went over to the liquor cabinet and got out a bottle of Scotch. I put it on the coffee table in front of him. Then I got glasses and ice and water and the new bottle of V.O. I bent over the table with my back to him and started making his Scotch and water.

"You're a cool one," he said from behind me. "It's a pleasure to have a contract like you."

I poured water into his Scotch and stirred it carefully. I straightened up and turned around. "Thanks," I said as I threw the drink, glass and all, into his face. At the same time I dropped to the floor.

The gun sounded like a cannon and something crashed across the room, but I didn't have time to see what it was. I was stretched out on the floor with my feet almost touching his. He was mopping at his eyes with one arm and swinging the gun down in my general direction. I hooked my right foot in back of his ankle, pulled on it, and at the same time kicked with my left foot at his kneecap. It's a good trick. If he'd been standing up, it would have broken his knee. As it was, it hurt, for he groaned and tried to twist away. I scrambled to a sitting position and chopped the edge of my hand across his wrist. The gun went skidding across the floor.

"That makes us a little more even," I said as I started to get to my feet.

He wasn't as much off balance as I'd thought. He leaned back on the couch and kicked with both feet. He caught me on the shoulder and sent me spinning across the room. I landed near where his gun had fallen.

He was already on his feet. For a second he stared wildly at me, but he must have seen that my hand was too near the gun for him to reach it first. Suddenly he turned and bolted for the door. He opened it and ran out before I could get the gun.

I stood up slowly and looked around the room. The bullet had hit the electric clock on my desk and pieces of it were all over the floor. There was more shattered glass by the couch. Everything else looked pretty normal.

I picked up his gun and put it on the desk. I got a dustpan and broom from the kitchenette and cleaned up the broken glass. Then I poured myself a stiff drink of V.O. I needed it.

I was just feeling better and getting ready to make a phone call when there was a knock on the door. I put down my glass and went over to it. I couldn't hear any noise from the hallway. I waited and then the knock came again.

"Mr. March," a voice said through the door, "this is Jameson, the super. Is everything all right?"

It was his voice, so I opened the door and looked out. "Is everything all right?" he repeated anxiously.

"Everything is fine," I said. "Why shouldn't it be?"

"One of the tenants," he said, "called down and said he heard an argument in here and then a shot."

"Oh that," I said. "I had the television set on and didn't realize that the volume was so high. I'm sorry."

"That's all?" he asked. He sounded disappointed.

"That's all," I said. "Tell the tenant I'm sorry. After this I'll turn on Lawrence Welk so he won't get so excited." I closed the door.

I went over and picked up the phone. I dialed a police number—a downtown office. When somebody answered, I asked for Lieutenant Johnny Rockland. I was told he'd already left, so I hung up and then dialed his home number. His wife answered and sounded resigned when I asked for him. A moment later he answered.

"Hi, Johnny," I said. "Milo."

"Hello, Milo," he said. "How's the insurance racket?"

"Like always. I want to ask you a couple of questions."

"It figures. You wouldn't be calling for social reasons. What is it?"

"Do you know a guy about five feet ten, very thin, almost emaciated? Has short-clipped white hair, although he's no more than about forty, and white-blue eyes. He—" I glanced at the desk—"carries a .38 automatic and uses it professionally. Does that ring any bells?"

"Sounds like Whitey Blake," he said, "although I haven't seen him around in a couple of years. Things got hot for him here five years ago and he went to Europe. The last I heard, he was supposed to be working with a gang over there."

"Could be the same boy," I said. "I think this one might be working for an international gang."

"What's the story, Milo?"

"No story. I don't even have an outline yet. I came home and found this guy waiting here with the idea of killing me. I didn't like the ending and changed the script, but he got away—leaving his gun behind."

"What are you working on?"

"Jewelry. I think it leads to Hong Kong."

"Maybe Whitey's back in town," he said. "I'll call the boys and see that word goes out to pick him up on sight. You say you have the gun?"

"That's right. You'll send somebody around for it?"

"Right away. Stick around." He hung up.

I put down the phone, and got busy with my packing for the trip. When everything was ready, I made myself another drink and sat down with a book. About an hour later there was a detective at the door. I gave him the gun and as much information as I could. Shortly after he left, I went to bed.

I was up early the next morning and into the office. Soon after I got there, a messenger arrived with an envelope for me. It was stuffed with money—a lovely sight. I checked with my answering service, but the only call I'd had was from Lieutenant Rockland. I had an idea it might be better if I didn't return it. I went out and picked up my reservation. Two hours later I was on a plane bound for Hong Kong.

Even though the plane was a jet, it was many hours later that it began to slip between the hills toward the airport on Kowloon. Looking down, the sea appeared to be a clear blue, flecked with gold. Beyond the stretch of water there was Hong Kong, the main part of it nestling between a steep hill and the sea, with tiers of houses running up the side of the hill.

"Your first trip to Hong Kong?" the Chinese beside me asked.

"Yes," I said.

"I find this the best part of the trip," he said. "I have made it many times, but there is always a feeling of excitement when the plane begins to glide between these hills. They are known, by the way, as the Nine Dragons, and even that conjures up dozens of pictures in my mind. Do you suppose I'm being ancestral?"

"I doubt it," I said with a smile. "I was just feeling pretty much the same way."

"A business trip?" he asked.

"Yes," I said. He was probably as harmless as he looked,

but there was no way to be sure and I wasn't volunteering anything.

"There's no place like it for business," he said. "There are so many people in Hong Kong that it seems a miracle they survive at all. Yet thousands more come over from the mainland every week, and somehow we put them to work and drum up more business somewhere in the world. We all manage to continue existing."

"As long as Mao decides to permit you," I said.

"Oh yes," he said cheerfully. "But that may be for some time. The mainland is like a man who must live under water. Hong Kong is the hollow bamboo through which he breathes." The wheels of the plane touched the ground. "May the gods of fortune smile on your visit to Hong Kong."

The plane rolled to a stop and we all filed out. The immigration office was a tiny place and we waited in a long, orderly line. The local policemen, neat in their navy serge uniforms with silver buttons, moved along the line and politely answered questions. Finally I was through and free to go. I took the ferry across to Hong Kong and then a taxi to the Far Eastern Hotel.

I registered and sent my bag up to my room with a bellboy. I asked directions to the nearest bank. It was just around the corner. I walked to it and changed my money into Hong Kong dollars. I went back to the hotel and up to my room. I called room service and ordered a bottle of V.O. and some ice. When it arrived, I poured myself a generous drink and sat down to look at the situation.

Hong Kong was my only clue. But now that I was here, I

didn't know where to look next. I had never been here before in my life, and the only thing I knew was that a girl named Mary Moy had supposedly taken a plane for the city. I'd certainly need help, and I had to start somewhere. I went downstairs and waited until the desk clerk finished registering a couple and turned his attention to me.

"Could you tell me where the police station is located?" I asked.

"I expect that would be the Central Station you'd want," he said. "You'll find it at Hollywood Road and Old Bailey Street. Is there anything wrong, sir?"

"Nothing wrong," I said. "I just like to visit police stations. That's my hobby."

"Really?" he said. "Well, I suppose that's not too unusual. I remember my grandfather once collected every newspaper story about Jack the Ripper. I recall seeing them around when I was a lad."

"Maybe he *was* Jack the Ripper," I suggested.

"Oh, I say!" the clerk exclaimed.

I left while the look of horror was still on his face. Outside, I hailed a taxi and gave the driver the address. When I got there, I showed all my papers and explained myself to a sergeant, and was finally shown in to see an Inspector John Simmons. I showed my papers and told my story again.

"Well," he said when I'd finished, "that's rather a tall order, you know. Is that all the information you have?"

"That's it," I said. "I'm hoping I'll be able to pick up more here."

He shook his head. "I don't like to discourage you, but it'll be quite a task. Do you know anyone in Hong Kong?"

"No."

"To begin with," he continued, "looking for a Mary Moy—even if that is her real name—will be like looking for a Mary Smith in New York. There are probably thousands, with more coming over from the mainland every day. And she may only have come through here on her way to some other spot."

"That's true," I admitted. "But I have to start somewhere. I thought I might get some help from you."

"What sort of help?"

"Information mostly. And I thought you might be able to find out if a Mary Moy did arrive on that plane from America."

"I can do that, I suppose. What else?"

"I'd like to find a good private detective who knows the city."

"I can give you a list of our private inquiry agents, but I'm afraid we can't recommend any particular one. It will merely be a list of those who have not broken any laws … so far as we know."

"I'll settle for that," I said. "And any other information which you may get."

"We shall do our duty as usual," he said stiffly. "We will look into the matter which you've brought to our attention. But I think you should understand, Mr. March, that if we do get any information as to criminals here, we shall act upon it ourselves and not turn it over to you."

"Sure," I said. "I don't care how much acting you do. I'm not interested in who gets the credit for what; I just want to see results."

"And I think you should know that if you come across any additional information, you must bring it to us. This would seem to be a police matter and not one for amateurs."

"A professional," I said pleasantly, "is one who gets paid for what he does. I get paid for doing my job on an international basis. You get paid for doing the same sort of work on a local basis. Let's get things clear, Inspector. I'm not planning on breaking any of your local laws. I will cooperate with you, but I don't expect to spend all my time at the cricket matches. Do I make myself clear?"

"Perfectly," he said coldly.

"Now," I said, "I'd like to know the name of any local man who is considered an expert on jade."

"There are probably several, but I believe the best is a Hsu Chin Kwang, a retired Chinese merchant. I've heard he has the largest collection of jade in the world."

"Thanks," I said. "Now, if you'll give me that list of private detectives, I'll run along."

He took a notebook and sheet of paper from his desk. He opened the book and copied from it. When he handed over the sheet of paper, there were six names on it.

"I must warn you, Mr. March," he said, "that Her Majesty's police do not look kindly on private citizens trying to take the law into their own hands. I trust you will keep that in mind."

"I'll keep it in mind," I said.

I went out and took another taxi back to the hotel. When I got there, I looked through the Hong Kong phone book. There was a number listed for Hsu Chin Kwang. I called it. Someone answered and I asked to speak to Mr. Hsu. I was told to wait.

After a minute another voice came on. This was a woman's voice, speaking cultivated English.

"This is Hsu Chin Kwang's daughter," she said. "Who is calling?"

"My name is Milo March. I represent an insurance company in America. I'm looking for information about jade and was told that your father is the foremost authority in Hong Kong. I'd like to talk to him."

"My father seldom speaks on the telephone," she said. "Will you wait a minute, please?" She was gone without waiting for me to answer.

She was back within a few minutes. "Mr. March," she said, "my father will see you tomorrow night. Be here at the house by eight o'clock."

"Where is the house?"

"Any taxi driver will be able to bring you to the house of Hsu Chin Kwang. Good day, Mr. March." There was a click as she hung up.

I looked at my watch. There was time enough to do one more thing before business was over for the day. I looked at the names the Inspector had given me. The first name on it was Frank Burney. I went downstairs and took a cab to the address.

It was located on a street lined with office buildings. The street itself was teeming with people, mostly Chinese, while cars inched their way through the crowd. I walked up a narrow stairway to a second-floor office. The sign on the door read: *Frank Burney & Associates, Ltd. — Confidential Inquiries.* I opened the door and went in.

The reception room was small and simply furnished, but it looked as if Frank Burney was doing all right. There was a pretty Chinese girl sitting behind a small desk. She looked up and smiled, waiting as I looked the room over.

"May I help you?" she asked when I finally turned to her. She spoke excellent English.

"I'd like to see Mr. Burney," I said.

"Who's calling, please?"

"Milo March."

She wrote it down in a book on her desk and looked up. "Your address?"

"New York City. I just arrived in Hong Kong today."

"Where are you staying in Hong Kong?"

"The Far Eastern Hotel."

She wrote that down and picked up her phone. She announced my name, listened for a couple of seconds, then replaced the phone. She gave me another smile. "You may go in, Mr. March," she said. "It's that door." She indicated the nearer of two doors that led out of the reception room.

I went through the door and into a moderately sized office. It was equipped with a desk and chair, two filing cabinets, and a more comfortable chair for a visitor. Two attractive Chinese prints hung on the walls. And back of the desk there was a big red-headed man with a typical Irish-American face. He stood up and held out his hand.

"Mr. March?"

I nodded and shook hands with him. "You're Frank Burney?"

"That's me," he said with a friendly grin.

"You look and sound like an American, too," I said, as I dropped into the chair in front of his desk.

"I am, although, God help me, I've been in Hong Kong for fifteen years. I keep telling myself that I'm going to quit and go back to the States next year, but all I've done is keep saying it for ten years. Well, maybe next year …"

"You sound like an addict," I said.

"It's not a bad town. You're new to Hong Kong?"

"Just got here today. You mean it shows?"

"Hong Kong is pretty insular," he said. "Most American and British residents know each other. How'd you happen to stumble across me?"

"I asked Inspector Simmons at the police to recommend a private detective. He gave me a list of six. Your name was at the top of the list, so I came here first."

"Old Simmons, eh? That's a switch. He doesn't care too much for private dicks."

"So I gathered," I said. "He did add that he couldn't actually recommend anyone, that the list was only those who hadn't done anything illegal so far as he knew."

"That sounds more like him. Well, what can I do for you, Mr. March? It isn't usual to need a private detective the first day in Hong Kong. Looking for someone?"

"In a way," I said. "I need someone who knows Hong Kong well, and especially someone who has access to information about what's going on in the underworld. There's a possibility that the case might get rough. Do you think you're my man?"

"I might be. What's the pitch?"

"I'm an insurance investigator. I'm on the trail of a stolen jade necklace. It was taken a little more than a week ago in New York. I believe that it was stolen by a man and woman, both Chinese, and that they came here. I have a name for the woman, but not the man. I think they are a part of a large gang operating out of Hong Kong. That's about the story." I deliberately left out the international angle. If he knew about that, he might want more money.

He swung around in his swivel chair and stared out through the window that looked down on the swarming street. After a minute, he swung back. "Do you mean the insurance company would be hiring us?"

I shook my head. "I'll be hiring you. The insurance company has hired me. I'll need help and I have an expense account to cover it."

"We could probably do the job for you," he said. "We don't handle too many criminal cases—no agency does here. But we do have a few Chinese operatives who have the sort of contacts you need. We certainly know the city. I've been here fifteen years and my partner has been here five. I've had my share of rough stuff when it was necessary. We can probably do as good a job as anyone else, maybe a little better." I liked his honesty.

"How much?" I asked.

"Two hundred dollars a day for each person used and, of course, our expenses." He must have noticed the expression on my face, for he smiled. "That's Hong Kong dollars."

I made a quick calculation. That was about thirty-five dollars a day—American dollars—for each person. "That'll be all right," I said, "as long as you don't suddenly put ten men on the payroll."

"We never pad our payroll or expenses," he said. "I think Simmons will tell you that much. Actually, either my partner or myself will work on the case alone, unless something comes up that requires someone else. Is it a deal?"

"It's a deal. Want some expense money in advance?"

"We usually get it."

"How much?"

"Five hundred dollars will do—Hong Kong dollars. We'll probably need more later, but we'll ask you. And, of course, we'll give you an accounting for what is spent."

I counted out five hundred dollars and gave it to him. He wrote out a receipt for me.

"Now," he said, "before you give me the rest of the information, I'd like you to meet my partner." He picked up his phone and pressed a button on its base. "Will you come in, Linda?" he asked. "There's someone I want you to meet." He replaced the phone.

A moment later the door opened and she came in. Even though I'd been warned by the name he had used, I wasn't prepared for what arrived. She was a blonde, probably in her late twenties, although she could have been younger. She had one of those flawless, beautiful faces that blondes sometimes have. And a figure that would have stopped traffic anywhere in the world.

"Linda," Burney said, "I'd like you to meet Mr. Milo March, a new client. Miss Linda McKay, my partner."

"I'm glad to know you, Mr. March," she said. She had a voice that went with the rest of her.

"Well," I said, "it seems to me that private detectives are

getting prettier every day. I'm sure the Pinkerton Agency was never like this."

They both laughed. "Linda's a damn good detective, too," Burney said, "although most people don't believe it when they first see her. ... Linda, I'll fill you in later on what Mr. March has already told me about his case. Now, Mr. March, you want to give us the details about the two people who pulled the job?"

"There isn't much to give," I said. "I know nothing about the man, except that he's Chinese. He showed up in New York two months ago and left a week ago, the day after the robbery. The safe was opened by an expert, and I think this man is the one who did it."

"That might be any one of a great number of men in Hong Kong," Burney said dryly. "We have a very high percentage of experts in all forms of crime."

"The girl called herself Mary Moy. She also arrived about two months ago and worked as a maid in the house that was robbed. She quit the job four days ago and caught a plane to Hong Kong."

"Any description of her?" the blonde asked.

"Only that she's young and beautiful and unusually tall for a Chinese girl."

"Did you tell Simmons about the case?" Burney asked.

"Yes. He said he'd try to check on it, and he warned me that he didn't care for what he called amateurs messing around in police cases."

"That sounds like him," Burney said. "Well, there isn't much to go on. What do you think, Linda?"

"From what I've heard," she said, "it sounds as if our best

bet might be to try to check on natives who have been away for the past two months and have just returned."

Burney nodded. "That, and see if we can pick up anything about a jade necklace. You know, March, there's also a possibility that your necklace has vanished over the bridge into Red China. There's considerable traffic both ways."

"I thought about it," I said.

"Okay," Burney said cheerfully, "we'll have a go at it."

"Either of you ever hear of a Whitey Blake?" I asked.

"Blake?" Burney repeated. "I don't recall the name. Is he in this?"

"I think so. He tried to kill me in New York."

Burney whistled. "He must be in something. We'll ask about him, too. And we'll keep you informed."

"There's one more thing," I told him. "I didn't come out here to sit in the hotel bar while you do all the work. I expect to be working on it, too."

"Fine," he said. "We'll try to scare up something and then we can all go to work."

"I'll hear from you, then," I said. I turned to the door.

"The minute we get something," he promised. "By the way, do you know anyone in Hong Kong?"

"Not a soul."

"I have an idea. Linda, why don't you show Mr. March around our city this evening?"

"I'd love to," she said, "but perhaps Mr. March has made other plans."

"If I have," I said, "you can consider them canceled as of now. Shall I pick you up in time for dinner?"

"I'd like that," she said. "Make it about seven. I'll write down my address for you." She went to the desk and wrote swiftly on a memo pad. She tore off the sheet and handed it to me.

I put it in my pocket, said good-bye, and left. When I got downstairs, I hailed a cab and went back to the hotel.

It was almost three hours before I had to pick up Linda McKay. I sat down in my room and had a drink first. I felt that I had at least made a start. I'd alerted the local police, hired a private detective, and made an appointment with a jade expert. I decided I'd earned the evening off.

When I finished my drink, I undressed and went into the bathroom. I shaved and showered and went back into the bedroom to dress. I had just slipped on my trousers when there was a knock on the door. I crossed the room and opened the door.

A Chinese stood there. It was difficult to guess his age, but he was probably no more than thirty. He was dressed in a tan silk suit with matching tie and handkerchief. There was a smile on his face.

"Mr. March?" he asked.

"Yes."

"My name is Jimmy Shan," he said. "I wonder if I might come in and talk to you for a minute?"

I opened the door wider and stepped to one side, so he could enter. I closed the door and looked at him. "I was about to have a drink," I said. "Will you join me?"

"With pleasure."

I poured two drinks and handed one to him. He took a sip and beamed.

"An excellent whiskey," he said. "I'm sure you and I will get along splendidly."

"Why?" I asked.

"It is a good question," he said solemnly. "As one of our ancient poets, Yuan Mei, said: 'One truth drives out a hundred shams.' We should get along well together because we have much to offer each other."

"Such as?"

"You have dollars to offer and I have my services."

"What kind of services?"

"Whatever you wish. I am a man of many talents—if you will pardon me for seeming to boast. I mention it only to explain."

"You haven't explained anything yet," I said. "Suppose you tell me which of your many talents you think I might need."

"The city of Hong Kong," he said, "is like a younger brother who tells me all of his secrets. Not a bug stirs without my notice. I know what is going on—down by the docks or up in the hills. If you desire that which is unobtainable, I can get it for you. If you desire a beautiful woman, I can find you the fairest of all. I know who keeps the shrine of Kuan Yin in a place of honor, and who has covered the face of Kuan Yin with a cloth so that she may not see the evil in their eyes."

"You sound like a man of many talents," I admitted, "but I don't think I am in dire need of any of the things you mention."

"Wait," he said. He held up the glass of whiskey so that the light would shine through it, and seemed to consult it. "I know that you, Mr. March, arrived in Hong Kong only today.

I know that you went to see the police and that you have hired a private detective. In both places you spoke of a jade necklace recently stolen in America. And I know that soon you will visit Hsu Chin Kwang, the retired merchant who collects jade."

I was startled, but managed not to show it too much. "You do get around, don't you?" I said. "How do you know these things?"

"It is my trade," he said modestly. "I, too, am a merchant, but my wares are information—and other things. For example, I believe that this is yours." He pulled a wallet from his coat. It was mine.

This time I didn't manage to conceal my surprise. I hadn't even known my wallet was missing. I reached over and took it from him. From a quick glance, it looked as if all the money was still in it.

"Where did you get this?" I asked.

"As you left the office of the private detective, a pickpocket took it from you. I jostled him in the crowd and recovered it for you."

"You could have picked my pocket yourself," I said.

"True," he admitted. "I could also have kept the wallet. From its thickness I would guess that it holds more money than I could earn by working for you."

He had a point there. "Why didn't you keep it?"

"Stealing does not interest me. It is beneath a man of my talents. I prefer to gather information and then say to myself, 'Who would be most interested in buying this?' This is the sort of work which I find entertaining—and profitable."

"Do you know where the jade necklace is?" I asked.

"No, but I might be able to find out."

"Do you know who Mary Moy is?"

"There are a thousand Mary Moys in Hong Kong. Perhaps I can find the one you speak of."

"And do you know anything about a gang of jewel thieves who operate from here?"

"I have heard," he said, "that there are some who go to other countries and return with valuable jewels. I have heard nothing about jade, but perhaps they take that, too."

"Do you know who they are?"

He shook his head. "A man was pointed out to me on the street once, and I was told that he was one of those who brought in the jewels, but I do not know."

"What was his name?"

"I do not remember. He was one of your people, an American, I think. He had white hair, although he was not an old man, and his eyes were like the caps on ocean waves. I do not remember anything else about him."

"Was his name Whitey Blake?"

"I do not remember. That sounds like the name, but I can't be sure."

"Can you find out more about him?"

"It is possible."

"How much do you want for your services?" I asked.

"You understand, Mr. March, I am not offering my full-time services. I have other interests which I must look after. So let us say ten dollars for each day. American dollars."

"Why American dollars?"

He smiled. "I can get more for them on the black market than the official rate of exchange."

"Well, you're honest about that at least," I said. "You sound as if you might be useful; but how do I know that you won't work for me and then also sell your services to those for whom I look?"

"It would be beneath my dignity," he said. "Besides, it is not good business."

"That sounds more like it," I said. "What did you say your name was?"

"Jimmy Shan."

"Okay, Jimmy. We'll try it for a few days and see what happens. If you produce, we'll continue. I'll pay you at the end of each day, starting tomorrow."

"That is satisfactory," he said. He finished his drink and stood up. "Now I will run along, as you will want to get ready for your date with Miss McKay."

"You know about that, too?"

"Oh yes. She is, as you would say, a doll. I trust it will be a pleasant evening. ... One thing more, Mr. March ..."

"Yes?"

"There are many here who make a living by prying secrets from Hong Kong and selling them. My chances of success will be greater if no one else knows about our arrangement."

"All right."

"I will see you tomorrow," he said. He crossed the room swiftly and was gone through the door.

I wondered about Jimmy Shan as I finished dressing. In a way, he seemed almost too good. It was always possible that he had been sent to lead me away from what I wanted. So I would use him—and watch him.

I'd already learned one lesson from him. On my way out, I stopped at the desk and had them put part of my money in the hotel safe. Then I went on to the address Linda McKay had given me.

It was a small but well-furnished apartment in one of the newer buildings. I had to wait while she finished dressing, and I wandered around the living room. One wall caught my eye. A whole section like a miniature bookcase had been built there, covering the wall from floor to ceiling. The shelves were filled with various Oriental figures, most of them made out of china, but some were stone and some were of flawed or cheap jade. Nevertheless, most of them were attractive, and I was still examining them when she came in ready to go.

We went to the Hong Kong Hotel for cocktails and dinner and afterwards to the Lai Chi Kok Club and danced. Except for the large number of Asian faces, we might as well have been back in New York. There was no conversation about business. We talked about all the little things that people do when they're getting acquainted. Later we took a ride around the city, past the public gardens with the fern trees looking like giant umbrellas and on out toward Victoria Peak. Once we got away from the main part of the city, the air was filled with the scent of frangipani and honeysuckle. It was very pleasant and romantic.

I took Linda home about one in the morning. I had the taxi wait while I walked her to her apartment.

"Thanks, Linda," I said at the apartment door, "for taking the time to show a tourist around. It was fun."

"It wasn't entirely altruistic," she said. "I had fun, too, Milo."

"Then we'll do it again."

"Tomorrow night?"

"I don't think so, honey," I said. "I have an appointment and I'm not sure how long it will take. But if not tomorrow night, then probably the night after that. If you're free."

"I will be," she said. "And if you do get through early tomorrow night, call me. Maybe you can come up for a drink."

I said good night and went back to the taxi. It was only a short ride to the hotel. I was tired and went straight up to my room. I unlocked the door and stepped inside, flicking on the light. I closed the door and turned around.

I took one step and stopped. The point of a knife was only a couple of inches from my belt buckle.

THREE

The knife was held by a large Chinese dressed in tattered pants and shirt. His face was slack, a thin line of spittle running from one corner of his mouth. His eyes were out of focus, the pupils dilated. From the way he held his body, I didn't think he was going to waste any time in idle conversation with me. He was already tensed to lunge forward, and I could feel my stomach trying to find someplace to hide.

There wasn't much of a choice. My gun was across the room in a dresser drawer beneath some shirts. I didn't want just to stand there, waiting to be stuck like a pig on the morning of a festival day. I took the only course left.

I slashed my left hand across his wrist, at the same time twisting my body as fast as I could. The blow didn't stop him, but it delayed his lunge by a fraction of a second. It was just enough. I felt a burning sensation along my belly and side, but I was still standing up and I had him where I wanted him. I grabbed his wrist with one hand and his elbow with the other, and shoved down as hard as I could. At the same moment I brought my knee up to meet his arm. There was a dull cracking sound and the breath whistled from his mouth. The knife dropped to the floor. His right arm flopped like an old sock.

His face twisting with pain, he started to bend over to pick up the knife with his left hand. I let him go partway, then brought my knee up again. It crashed into his cheekbone and straightened him up. I hit him with a right as hard as I could. He staggered, but didn't go down. I started to move in on him and he suddenly lowered his head and charged. I sidestepped and hit him in the broken arm. His breath came out in a high-pitched squeal.

For a minute he stood there, staring at me, the one arm flapping at his side. His breath continued to make a noise in his throat. I took a step toward him. His gaze flicked down to the knife on the floor, then back to me—and he broke. He turned and clawed at the door until he got it open. He ran down the empty corridor, sobbing.

I closed the door. Leaving the knife on the floor, I ripped off my coat and shirt and looked at my side. The damage was slight. There was a red streak across half of my stomach and across my ribs. It wasn't deep, but there was still some blood oozing from it, and it would be sore for a few days. I went into the bathroom and put cold water on it until the bleeding stopped. I didn't have any bandages, but I did have some iodine, and I smeared that on it. It stung as it bit into the wound.

I had just gone back to the bedroom when there was a light knock on the door. I looked at my watch. It was almost two in the morning. I picked the knife up from the floor and tossed it on the dresser. I went to the door expecting to see the desk clerk or the house detective. It was Jimmy Shan.

"You are all right?" he asked as I looked out.

"Why shouldn't I be?" I asked. I didn't like the coincidence of his appearance.

"I just saw someone I know running from the hotel," he said. "His arm was broken, and he looked as if he'd been in a fight. He is not one I would expect to see in this hotel, so I thought at once he had been here."

"Come in," I said wearily, opening the door wider. I closed the door as soon as he was inside. "You seem to have a habit of catching me with my shirt off. Now, who was your friend?"

His quick glance had already taken in the knife on the dresser and the streak around my middle. "He is not a friend," he said gravely. "His name is Chan Chok How and he is a common thief. He was waiting for you when you came home?"

"Yes," I said. "But what I want to know is how you came to be downstairs and saw him run out."

"I just happened to be in the neighborhood," he said blandly. "You suspect me of having something to do with his visit to you?"

"The idea had crossed my mind," I admitted.

"You are wrong, Mr. March," he said. He smiled. "If I wanted to do away with you—and where, then, would I find ten dollars per day?—I would do it myself and not hire such a one as Chan Chok How. To begin with, he belongs to the old ones who still believe in steel because it is quiet and does not quickly bring the police. I would rather depend on a gun and then on my own speed to leave before the police arrive. You see, I am modern."

"I see," I said dryly. "That makes it impossible for you to be involved in the attack upon me?"

"Of course," he said simply. "You are not badly hurt?"

"Just a scratch."

"You must be a good man," he said. "Chan Chok How is said to be clever with a knife. He is strong as an ox—and very brave when he has had his opium."

"I'd rather know who sent him. Is that included in your great store of information?"

"Not at the moment. Perhaps I can find out tomorrow. It might be almost anyone. Do you know Po Hing?"

"Never heard of him. Why?"

"It is for Po Hing that Chan Chok How usually works. Po Hing runs a most profitable business, stealing goods from the ships in the harbor and then selling them in Europe. If you had crossed Po Hing in some manner, then I would say that he might have sent Chan Chok How."

"Does your Po Hing also steal jewelry?"

"Not to my knowledge. He deals in everything from a camera to a ship itself, but I do not believe he has ever touched jewelry. But Chan Chok How could have been working for someone else. A job on the side, you might say."

"Who?"

"That I cannot say immediately. I have never heard of him working for anyone else, but I will ask questions tomorrow. Tomorrow Chan Chok How will not feel well. Perhaps he will even talk for a fresh pipe of opium."

"Then make him," I said. "I'll pay for the opium. But I want to know who sent him."

"I will do my best," he said. "Is there anything I can do for you before I leave?"

"No," I said. "I'll see you tomorrow."

"Good night," he said, and opened the door.

"Good night."

As soon as he was gone, I had myself a final drink and went to bed. I was tired and fell asleep at once.

I didn't wake up until about ten. I called downstairs and ordered some breakfast. Then I went into the bathroom for a fast shower. I looked at my wound. It was sore as hell, but it seemed to be all right. At least there was no sign of infection. I padded back into the bedroom and tossed the knife into a dresser drawer. There was no point in leaving it out for the inspection of bellboys and maids. I put on my robe, made sure the door was unlocked, and got back into bed. I lit my first cigarette of the day.

There was a knock on the door. I called out and the waiter opened the door and came in, wheeling a small table before him. He brought it over to the bed and arranged it.

I checked to be sure that everything was there. It was. Ham and eggs and soft rolls with plenty of butter. A big pot of coffee. Orange juice. And a bucket of ice. I took the bill, added the tip, and signed it. I handed it back to the waiter. He glanced at the size of the tip before he said anything.

"Thank you, sir," he said then. He nudged something on the table. "The desk asked me to bring this up with your breakfast, sir."

"Thanks," I said. I could see it was a cablegram. I waited until he left, then picked it up and tore it open. I glanced at the bottom first. It was from Lieutenant Johnny Rockland.

I DON'T KNOW IF IT'S THE YEAR OF THE RAT WHERE YOU ARE,

BUT IT SHOULD BE IF YOU'RE THERE. WE PICKED UP YOUR VISITOR BUT HAD TO RELEASE HIM, SINCE YOU ARE THE ONLY WITNESS. HOPE HE FINDS YOU.

JOHN ROCKAND

I laughed and tossed it on the night table. It had been a dirty trick to play on Johnny, but staying in New York might have delayed my trip by a week or more. And it might help my case if Whitey Blake did show up in Hong Kong while I was there.

I had a good shot of V.O. with my orange juice and then tackled the eggs. I was on my second cup of coffee when there was another knock on the door. Thinking it was the waiter returning for the table, I called for him to come in.

It was Jimmy Shan.

"Good morning," he said cheerfully. "How are you feeling this morning?"

"All right—until just now," I said. "I thought I was hiring you on a part-time basis, but it's beginning to feel as if I'd adopted you."

"I came early," he said, "because, as the poet Yuan Mei said, 'Late in the day the flowers are not at their best.' The same might be said of information."

"You brought something other than a gem from your favorite poet? You've talked to my would-be assassin already?"

He shook his head and brought a folded Chinese newspaper out from beneath his arm. "No, I came to report that it will not be possible for me to question Chan Chok How about his employer."

"Why not?"

"Early this morning the body of Chan Chok How was pulled from the water by the police near the Ping An wharf. He was dead. Drowned. But since he had a broken arm and several bruises, the police are suspecting that it was not an accident."

"There's a story in the paper?" I asked.

He nodded.

"Let me see." I held out my hand for the paper.

"You read my language?" he asked as he handed it over.

"Pu ts'ui," I said impatiently. I looked up at him and smiled. "I'm glad to see there's one thing you didn't know about me."

I turned my attention back to the paper. But he had given me the whole story. There was nothing else in it except a description of the man and the fact that the police suspected him of being a criminal murdered in an argument over a division of the spoils.

"What do you think?" I asked, handing back the paper.

"Someone demanded payment for failure," he said. "Whoever hired him must have realized that he was the weak link to them. They killed him and destroyed the link. It is an old solution to an older problem."

"I suppose so."

"I spoke this morning," he said, "to a man who worked on the waterfront with Chan Chok How. He told me that Chan had confided in him that he was going on a different job last night. He was warned that Po Hing might be angry if he stole for himself or for another, and Chan said that this was a different job. He bragged that he was to be paid many dollars for using his knife."

"That was all?"

He nodded. "Chan said nothing that would indicate who was paying him for the job. It would seem that there is no longer an avenue from that direction. We must look elsewhere."

"I got the message," I said. "Do you remember that yesterday I asked you if the man who was once pointed out to you was named Whitey Blake?"

"Yes."

"Well, I want you especially to try to find out about him. I believe that he may be coming back to Hong Kong, perhaps today or tomorrow. I'd like to know about it when he arrives. At least in him we have something more specific to look for than with a Mary Moy and an unnamed Chinese burglar."

"I will work on it at once."

"Good," I said. "Now, as much as your conversation delights me, I don't want to keep you from your other interests. I believe that you mentioned having several."

He took the hint and left, promising to see me soon. I was sure he'd keep the promise. The problem was likely to become one of finding a way not to see him so often.

I got up and slowly dressed and went downstairs. I bought a number of English-language newspapers and sat in the lobby, scanning them quickly. There was nothing that hadn't been in the Chinese paper.

When I'd finished with the papers, I went to the phone and called Frank Burney. He didn't have much to tell me. He hadn't found out anything about Whitey Blake. He had called a man who sometimes worked for him, and had him trying to run down something on the jewelry angle. The contact had told him that he'd heard rumors that a Po Hing was stealing jewelry, and he was going to check on it. Burney explained to me that Po Hing was a well-known Hong Kong thief. I didn't say anything about having heard the name.

After that I went out and found a taxi. I told the driver that I wanted to go to the Chinese section. He nodded and we were off. It wasn't far away. He let me out on the corner of a narrow winding street, and I was on my own.

Cities have a personality just as people do. Even when it's a completely alien city, there's a feeling about every part of it. Hong Kong was no different. I started down a street that was jammed with stores of all kinds, selling everything from magic herbs to modern watches and tailored suits. It was bustling with business, both native and tourist. Almost every shop had a small statue in the door, the earth god who is supposed to protect the establishment. It was a street of more or less honest businesses; you could sense that about it.

But within a couple of blocks there was a change. There was something more furtive about the shops, an air of making you believe that there were even greater bargains—although perhaps illegal—just the other side of the door. The women on the street were different. They were still Chinese and still female, maybe more so than the ones on the other streets, but there was a difference in the way they swung their hips. They were professionals. This was the section I was looking for.

Every city has a section like this, an area that's a jungle. A section where there's larceny in every heart, and where the inhabitants can count the money in your pocket right through the cloth. It doesn't look so much different from the other parts of the city, but you can smell and feel the difference just the same.

I wandered down the street until I came to what looked like a pawn shop. Much of the goods were displayed in front of the shop, and they included everything from cheap jewelry to an old battered piano. A scrawny Chinese with a wispy mustache stood in front of the store. He had already sized me up without seeming to before I reached him.

I stopped and looked at the jewelry.

"Very fine jewels," he said. "Will sell cheap. Maybe twenty-five dollars."

The stuff I was looking at wasn't even as good as you could find in a five-and-ten. I held up a necklace. "A man would be ashamed to carry such a thing home," I said in Chinese. He was startled, and I could see him taking a second look at me. "Don't you have something which would not make me an object of shame to my ancestors?"

"Oh, yes," he said in his own language. "I have many valuable stones inside, if you would consent to step into my humble store."

"What kind of stones?" I asked.

"Very fine ones. Would you care to look at them?"

"No," I said. "I know the jewels that I want, and you do not have them."

"I do not understand," he said.

"It is a simple matter. I am looking for someone who will secure for me the jewels I want."

"You mean buy them for you?"

"Did I mention buying?" I said. "I said someone who could secure them for me. Would you know such a man?"

"Ah," he said. "It is a difficult thing you request …"

"Do you know Po Hing?" I asked.

His gaze flickered away, then back to me. "I do not remember the name."

"I have heard that he might be the one for whom I search, but I do not know where he is to be found. I thought you might know."

"No," he said uncertainly. Greed struggled with suspicion in his eyes.

"Well," I said, "I will pass by another day. Perhaps you will think of someone who will help me."

"Perhaps. I will put my thoughts to your problem. Is there a place where one can reach you?"

"Sure," I said. "The Far Eastern Hotel. My name is Milo March. But I will pass this way again."

He bowed and I walked on. Twice more I stopped at places and asked similar questions, each time bringing up the name of Po Hing. I didn't get any better answers than at the first place, but I was satisfied. I had a good idea that word that I was asking about Po Hing would get back to him. Then there might be some action. It was a method that had often worked for me.

I went back to the hotel and spent the rest of the day there. In the evening Jimmy Shan showed up to collect his ten dollars for the day, but he had nothing to report. I had dinner in the hotel. Later I got a taxi and directed the driver to take me to the house of Hsu Chin Kwang. We were soon following the winding road up toward Victoria Peak.

It was an imposing house on one of the terraced levels on the side of the mountain. The taxi let me out in front of it, and I went up and rang the bell. The door was opened by a servant.

"Hsu Chin Kwang," I said. "I am Milo March and I'm expected."

"Come in, please," he said.

I followed him down the hallway and into a room. The servant announced me in Chinese and left. But I had stopped paying any attention to him.

There was a girl in the room. A beautiful girl. She had classic Chinese features. She wore a modern dress, with the high collar and the slit skirt, that revealed her figure to be just as classic.

"Mr. March?" she said.

I nodded.

"I am the daughter of Hsu Chin Kwang," she said. "I will take you to my father, but I thought first I should tell you that while he speaks English, he does not think well in the language so that his answers may sometimes seem slow."

"There's no problem," I said. "I speak Chinese."

"Mandarin?" she asked.

"Yes. And Cantonese."

"That is unusual for an American," she said. "May I ask why?"

"Sure," I said. "I was first taught by the United States Army. Then I was one of the first men sent in to help drive the Japanese out of China, so I got more practical training in the language."

"I see," she said. "Come. I will take you to my father."

"Aren't you joining us?" I asked as I followed her from the room.

"No," she said. "My father is quite old and he clings to many of the old ways of our people. He does not believe that women should be present when men are conversing."

We came to another door. She tapped on it lightly, then opened it. She addressed her father with traditional respect, and told him that I was there and that I spoke Chinese. She withdrew from the doorway, leaving me to enter.

It was a large room, with the furnishings strictly Chinese. I finally spotted Hsu Chin Kwang on the far side of the room. He wore black silk pants and jacket. The only modern thing about him was the cigarette he was smoking. His hair was white, as was his long, sparse beard. The years had deeply lined his face, so that he resembled an old Chinese brush drawing.

I spoke to him formally, thanking him for the honor of permitting me to visit him.

"March *hsien*," he said, "you have honored my home. It is a double honor, since you not only speak my language but understand the old ways. Too many of my own people no longer care to express themselves properly. Please be seated." I took a seat near him.

"You will have tea with me?" he asked.

I said that I would. He clapped his hands sharply, and another servant appeared through the door with tea. It was served. After I had tasted it, I complimented him on it and finally felt I could broach my reason for being there.

"I am told," I said, "that you are the foremost authority on jade. This is why I have come to see you."

"You pay me compliments which I do not deserve, March *hsien*. I am only a poor student of jade, but I will be happy to share what little knowledge I have with you. You are a lover of jade?"

"I don't know," I said honestly. "I've liked the few pieces I've seen, but I know little about it."

"A pity. It is one of the most beautiful of stones. The old name for it in my country was *yu*. That which was most ancient, having been passed from generation to generation, was called *ke yu*. Old jade which had been mined was known as *chin yu,* while that which had been buried with the dead was *han yu*. The name *jade* came from your own country, as you probably know."

"I didn't know it," I said.

"Oh, yes. When the Spanish explorers first went to America, they found the Indians using jade to ward off sickness. The explorers called the stone *piedra de ijada*. Later the French called it *pierre de l'éjade* and later shortened it to *le jade,* and from this came the present name."

"But you had it long before that," I said.

He nodded. "We know of jade which dates back to what you would call 1700 B.C. The Shang dynasty ruled then. I myself have a few pieces from that period. Jade has long been loved by the Chinese. Confucius compared it to virtue. He said: 'It is warm, liquid, strong and firm like politeness. Like the truth it gives out a bright rainbow.' "

"That's very interesting," I said. It wasn't really what I wanted to know, but I thought it better to let him talk.

"In the old days the symbol of China was the jade seal, and even in the Republic the highest order was the Order of Brilliant Jade."

"I understand," I said, "that you have one of the largest and best collections of jade in the world."

"I have a small collection," he said. "I have only a few things from the Shang dynasty, a few more from the Chou dynasty, and several from the Ch'en and Han dynasties. I think I am especially fond of that vase up there." He pointed to a vase on a mantel against the wall. It was a large white vase with a cover and two strap handles. It was covered with figures.

"You will notice," he said, "that it has the conventional *fao t'ieh* masks and that the handles have the dragon heads."

I murmured the proper things.

"But I talk too much," he said. "I am an old man and sometimes I forget that water runs faster from a barren hill than from one that is young and vigorous. You will forgive me? You came to see me for a purpose and I am not permitting you to state it."

"But I enjoyed what you have said," I protested. "It is also true that I came to seek your help upon a matter involving jade."

"My limited knowledge is at your disposal."

"As I have said, you are known to have one of the largest and best collections of jade in the world. Are you familiar with other large collections?"

"I know about some of them, although I have not seen them."

"Do you also know," I asked, "that there have been many valuable pieces of jade disappearing during the past year or so? All from different parts of the world."

"You mean stolen?"

"Yes."

"I have heard of this," he said, "but I'm afraid that I know very little of the matter. Valuable property is always being stolen, when it is not well guarded."

"But are you also aware that these pieces of jade have not shown up after being stolen? Other things stolen by the same people are eventually sold and can be found. But the jade does not appear again."

"Ah," he said. He stared at me, his eyes dulled with age yet full of wisdom. "It has occurred to you that since the jade does not reappear, it is all ending up in the hands of a collector?"

"That is one idea," I said. "I thought you might know other large collectors well enough to tell me if one of them might be that greedy."

"It might even be myself," he suggested.

"True," I admitted. "I have thought of that."

"I am very wealthy and also very old. I cannot take the money with me when I go to join my ancestors, so why should I have things stolen when I can buy them?"

"I imagine that would also apply to the other collectors," I said. "Perhaps the desired pieces of jade were not for sale."

"That is possible," he said, nodding his head. "Nothing in my own collection is for sale. I'm sure that it is true of other collections around the world."

"Are there any special pieces owned by others which you've tried and failed to buy?"

He smiled. "Not in recent years, March *hsien*. A man does not live long enough to collect all that he desires."

"Have there been any attempts to steal any of your jade?"

"I do not know. There have been men who tried to rob me, many men throughout the years. The police can tell you more than I can about them. But none has succeeded, so I cannot tell you exactly what they desired."

"I was hoping," I said, "that you might be able to tell me which collectors might be willing to go beyond the law to add to their collection."

"I am sorry I cannot," he said. "I do not know any of the collectors. While your theory may be right, perhaps you should also look elsewhere. Perhaps someone new to jade, who has never collected before. Such a person might find it difficult to buy what he wants."

"I had thought of that," I said.

"I believe you also mentioned the possibility of another idea. Do you mind telling an old man what it is?"

"No. Some group may be stealing the jade and taking it into Red China."

"Restoring national treasure to the people? Yes, I suppose that might be possible. If it is, I imagine that would make it much more difficult to recover it."

"That is certainly true."

"I suppose, March *hsien,* that your interest in the jade is to recover it?"

"Yes," I said.

"I am sorry that I cannot help you," he said. "When I was much younger, I was not always careful about where my wealth came from; but I discovered, since acquiring property, that I now believe it should be protected. If I hear anything concerning the jade, I shall inform you."

It was clearly a dismissal. I thanked him for his time, praised his tea and his house, and bowed myself out. I was barely in the hall when I was again joined by his daughter.

"My father talked with you for a long time," she said. "He must have been pleased by your visit. It is unfortunate that he could not tell you what you wished to know."

I looked at her in surprise. "How did you know?"

"I was listening from the next room," she said. She smiled at my expression. "No, my father did not know and would not approve. He believes that a woman should only be decorative. I have been a big disappointment to him. He had three daughters by his first wife, then divorced her and married my mother. When I was born, I believe he resigned himself to the fact that the gods did not intend him to have a son."

"I think it would be impossible to improve over the present result," I said.

"Thank you, Mr. March."

"You have one advantage over me," I told her. "I know that you are his daughter, but I don't know your name."

"Mei Hsu. You see, I am modern and arrange my name in the Western fashion. My father does not approve of it."

"Well, I do," I said. "Do you know anything about your father's jade collection?"

"Sometimes I help to arrange the pieces, but I know only what he thinks I am worthy of being told."

We had reached the front of the house. I glanced at my watch and was surprised to see that I had been there well over an hour. "May I phone for a taxi?" I asked.

"I believe one is waiting for you," she said. "When I knew your conversation with my father was almost over, I made the call for you."

"Thanks," I said. "Do you always anticipate what a man is going to want?"

"Often," she said. She looked at me and smiled, and there were impish lights in her black eyes. "For example, you are about to tell me that you would like to see me again, perhaps to suggest that I show you around Hong Kong."

She was right, and there was no point in playing games about it. "How did you know?"

"There is something in a man's eyes when he is about to say such a thing to a woman."

"Okay," I said. "As a matter of fact, I was going to tell you that I'm very fond of Chinese food—which is true—but I don't like tourist traps. Any suggestions?"

"Have you ever been to the boat restaurants of Aberdeen?"

"No."

"I think you will like them."

"Will you go with me?" I asked.

She nodded. "My father would not approve, but I will go."

"I'm glad he doesn't have much influence," I said. "Tomorrow night?"

"Yes."

"Good. Shall I pick you up here?"

"You do not have a car, do you?" she asked.

"I will have by tomorrow night. Here at about seven?"

"That will be fine." She opened the door. "Good night, Mr. March."

She was right about the taxi, too. It was waiting in front of the house. I said good night and left. The taxi took me directly back to the hotel.

I stood in front of the hotel for a minute, undecided what to do. It was still early. Finally, I made up my mind to go and phone Linda. If she wasn't busy, maybe we could sit around and have a few drinks. I turned to go in, and found the way barred by a burly Chinese. He was well dressed, but the suit wasn't tailored well enough to conceal completely the outlines of the gun he wore under one arm.

"Are you," he asked in Chinese, "the foreign devil who is called Milo March?"

"*Shih,*" I admitted.

"You are to come with me."

"Where?"

He showed his teeth in a wide smile. "Po Hing. It is said that you were looking for him only today. I have come to take you to him."

FOUR

There was a minute or so when I didn't know what to do. I didn't have a gun on me—or a permit to carry the gun that was up in my room. There were plenty of people on the street, but none of them was paying any attention to me. On the other hand, I told myself, this was what I'd been asking for. I had gone into the criminal section of Hong Kong and asked about Po Hing. I'd done it in order to force him to make a move. What had I expected—a box of chocolates? I said to hell with it and returned the smile of the big man.

"I am ready," I said. "How do we go?"

"I have a car," he said. "Come."

I went with him down the street. The car, a small European make, was parked about a block away. There was another Chinese at the wheel. I climbed in the back, followed by the man who had accosted me.

The car was soon winding up into the hills in the same general direction from which I had just returned. But it turned off and stopped in front of a house on a lower terrace. It certainly wasn't so big a house as the one I had visited earlier, but it did show that Po Hing, whatever he was doing, was making a buck.

The big Chinese and I went up to the house. He escorted me to a room off in one wing. In it was a fat Chinese, dressed in an expensive silk suit.

"This is the one called March," my escort said.

The fat Chinese looked at me. "You speak my language?" he asked.

"Yes."

"I also speak American," he said, switching to it. "I was born in San Francisco and stayed there until I got smart. There I was Peter Po and worked in my father's laundry; here I am Po Hing and you can see for yourself. Want a drink?"

"I never refuse one," I said.

"What kind?"

"Whatever you're having."

He snapped out an order to the man who had brought me in, and a moment later there were two glasses, ice, soda, water, and a bottle of V.O. on the table. Po Hing poured himself a half glass of whiskey and motioned me to help myself. Not to be outdone, I poured the same amount.

"So you're Po Hing," I said.

He smiled as broadly as if I'd identified him as a movie star. "This afternoon you were in the Wan Tsai District. Yes?"

"If you say so. I was wandering around Hong Kong, but I don't know the names of the districts."

"You asked about jewelry?"

"I think I showed some interest in jewelry at one place."

"You also asked about Po Hing?"

"I seem to remember something of the sort," I said.

He took a long drink and stared at me over the rim of the glass. "What is your racket, March?"

"What do you mean?"

"You know what I mean," he said. He lit a cigarette. "I am

well known in Hong Kong. Ask anyone, from a beggar on the docks to the police, and he will be able to tell you that he knows of Po Hing. He may also tell you that I am a thief. Many people have called me a thief, but no one has ever proved it in a court. You understand?"

"Yeah," I said. "You've always beaten the rap."

"That's right, I've always beaten the rap," he said. He smiled and pounded his chest. "Always. Lots of people have called me a thief. They said that I stole food, that I stole radios and watches, that I stole cars and factory machinery—but nobody ever said that I stole jewelry. Maybe I never had the chance. Then you come along, all the way from America, and you say that you want some jewelry stolen and that you hear that I'm the man to do it. Why? Did someone really tell you to see Po Hing, or did you make that up?"

I decided to play it as honest as I could. "I made it up."

"I thought so," he said. He was pleased with himself. "You made it up so that I would send for you—just as I did. Right?"

"Right."

"Good. We get somewhere. Now I ask you the question again. What is your racket?"

"I'm looking for some jade," I said.

He shrugged. "Who isn't? That's like saying you're looking for money. Do you mean that you want some special jade and that you want to hire me to steal it?"

"No. This jade has already been stolen. I want to get it back."

"Cop?"

"You might call me one, but I'm not. I work for an insurance company."

"You're offering a reward for the jade?" he asked.

"No," I said honestly. "I might, if I decide it's worth it. Right now I'm expecting to get all the rewards myself."

"An honest answer," he said approvingly. "But it is not what I first asked. Why do you use the name of Po Hing in the street, so that you will be brought to see me?"

"Chan Chok How," I said.

He switched his gaze to the burly Chinese who was still standing beside the table. "Do I know Chan Chok How?" he asked in Chinese.

"You know him," the man answered in the same language. "You threatened to beat him many times because he was stupid."

"Ai," Po Hing said. He returned to English. "He's the one who was fished from the water this morning like a hooked lentjan. The police say he was murdered. But what does he have to do with this? He was stupid. There is nothing worse than a stupid thief."

"He tried to kill me last night in my hotel," I said.

"So he failed—he was too stupid even to kill well, that one—and you then killed him."

"No. I broke his arm, but I did not kill him."

"Then I don't understand why you are here. It is well that he is dead. He won't try to kill you again."

"I want to know who sent him to kill me," I said.

"Oh ..."

"I arrived in Hong Kong yesterday to look for some jade," I said. "So far as I know, no one knew I was coming here. I don't know anyone in Hong Kong—or didn't before I arrived.

But the first night I was here, Chan Chok How came around to kill me. Someone had to send him. He worked for you."

"Oh-ho," Po Hing said. He laughed, but there was little merriment in his eyes. "Clever, these Occidentals. You arrive in Hong Kong looking for jade; Chan Chok How arrives in your room to kill you. Chan Chok How sometimes worked for me. Therefore you arrive here to accuse me of stealing the jade and trying to have you killed—and, failing in that, killing Chan Chok How instead."

"It could have been that way," I agreed.

"Have another drink," he said. "I like you. You have guts. You came here thinking I did all that. Then why wouldn't I just kill you when you got here and dump you in the same waters?"

I poured myself a drink and sipped it. "First," I said, "you don't know that I didn't arrange to be followed, if I were picked up. Secondly, I don't kill easily."

For the first time he looked at me with speculation. "I believe you. I have known men like that. I wonder if you— but, no. We must not mix business with pleasure." He looked at the other man. "What did we do last night?"

"Macao wharf," the other answered. "We did not need Chan Chok How. He said that he had another job."

"Did he talk about it?"

"No, except to say that he would be wealthy."

Po Hing turned back to me. "Chan Chok How was not working for me last night. Sometimes he did not work for me for days at a time. And I can only say that if I sent someone to kill you—or anyone else—it would not be such a stupid one as Chan Chok How."

I was beginning to believe he was telling the truth. "Maybe," I said.

"You are looking for some jade that was stolen in America?" he asked.

"Yes."

"And for the employer of Chan Chok How, when he tried to kill you last night?"

"Yes."

"And you think that one person might be the answer to both questions," he said. He gave me the smile again. "Okay. I will look for that person. If I find him, I may tell you for a price."

"You mean," I said evenly, "if the price I offer is higher than you can get anywhere else?"

His smile became broader. "You are a man of the world. We will get along okay. I will send for you when I have something to sell."

It was a dismissal. I finished the drink in my glass and got up. The burly Chinese and I went out together. A few minutes later he dropped me off in front of my hotel. I walked into the lobby and spotted a familiar face. Jimmy Shan's.

"You are all right?" he exclaimed, hurrying up to me.

"I'm all right," I said. "But aren't you working overtime?"

"I will not charge you for it," he said seriously. "I saw you picked up by one of Po Hing's men, and I could not leave until I knew you were all right."

"You saw me picked up? Where were you?"

"I just happened to be in the neighborhood ..."

"Just happened?" I said. "A likely story. And what did you

do when you saw me picked up? Rush in and soothe your shattered nerves with a drink?"

"I waited to see what would happen. If you hadn't returned within a reasonable time, I would have called the police."

"Great," I said. "That might have done me a lot of good. And what would you have done if the police arrived at Po Hing's too late?"

"I would have agreed," he said gravely, "with the poet Yuan Mei that 'in the casual life of meetings and partings there is much sadness to endure.' "

"Well," I said, "at least I get poetry for my money, if nothing else. But I'd still like to know how you just happened to be around here."

"I had come to tell you that I thought you were making a mistake."

"How?"

"This afternoon you walked into the Wan Tsai District and mentioned the name of Po Hing. This might have made him very angry. But now it seems that he was not too angry."

"Isn't that nice?" I said. "I don't know what I'd do without you, Jimmy, but I'd like to find out. Good night, if that's not too much of a strain on your services."

"Good night," he said cheerfully, and left.

So I found out what I'd do without him. I called Linda McKay and went over to her apartment. She had the drinks all ready when I got there. I sat in a comfortable chair and let her put a glass in my hand. First, I tried to talk about business, but she didn't know anything to tell me. She wasn't working on my case, and Burney had still been out of the office when she left. So I gave up and turned to more pleasant topics.

There came a time—doesn't it always?—when I'd had enough to drink and the conversation had slowed down, so I made a pass. She knocked it down before it even got under way.

"I'm sorry, Milo," she said. "I enjoyed being out with you last night and it's fun just sitting here and talking tonight. Let's leave it that way."

"Why?" I asked. "A boyfriend?"

She shook her head. "No boyfriend."

"You disapprove of the oldest obsession in the world—unless it comes complete with a license and old shoes and rice?"

"Not exactly that either," she said slowly. "I guess if I liked a guy well enough, that wouldn't stand in the way. But I met you only yesterday, and tomorrow you may be on your way back to New York. I like you well enough to spend some time with you, but let's say that at the moment I don't want to make a bigger investment."

I lit two cigarettes and handed one to her. "At least it's an honest answer," I said. "Okay, honey, we'll play it your way, but if there's ever a change in the house rules, let me know."

"I'll send you an engraved invitation," she said. "Man wanted. Come quickly."

I laughed. "No references needed? Sounds like just what I've been looking for." With that, I dropped it and we went back to drinking and talking. Finally, about two in the morning, I went back to the hotel feeling virtuous as hell.

I was up the next morning at nine. While I was having my coffee, I phoned Frank Burney. The girl said he'd just come in, and a moment later he was on the phone.

"Good morning," he said cheerfully. "Getting itchy?"

"A little," I admitted. "I know you've only been on the job for one day and that isn't much time. But I'm not used to just sitting around, so I thought I'd get in touch."

"I do have one little thing for you. That Whitey Blake you asked about. My information is that he's been away, but is due back in Hong Kong today."

"Know what flight he'll be on?"

"No."

"Got an address for him?"

"Not yet, but I have a man digging on it. Should have something before long. I did learn that Blake is known as a sharp operator, but he's never been in any brush with the law here."

"Anything on jade thieves yet?"

"Not a whisper, but I've got all my lines out. Ought to have something in a few days."

"All right," I said. "We'll keep in touch."

I hung up and went back to my coffee. I had just finished it when there was a knock on the door. I looked at my watch and made a mental bet with myself.

"The door's unlocked," I called. "Come in, Jimmy."

The door opened. I was right. It was Jimmy Shan. There was a big smile on his face. I didn't return it. Maybe I was too impatient, but I was beginning to feel I had a lot of employees without any work getting done.

"I trust," I said, "that the smile means that you have good

news, in addition to the fact that it's another day and therefore more money for you?"

"There is good news," he said. "I have found out about your Whitey Blake. Today he returns to Hong Kong."

"I already know that. Is that all you found out? When does he return? Where will he be in Hong Kong? What about his connections with jewelry thefts?"

"I don't know where he is coming from," Jimmy Shan said. "If I had known that, I could have found out from Pan American when he might arrive."

"That's right," I said. I picked up the phone and asked the operator to get me Pan American. When I got the information clerk, I asked about planes arriving from America with connections to New York. There were two arriving late that afternoon. I replaced the receiver and looked at Jimmy.

"Well, that's some sort of beginning," I admitted. "There are two planes arriving today. I guess I can meet both of them and, when I spot Whitey, trail him to wherever he is going."

"Even that is not necessary," Jimmy said. "I have learned where Whitey Blake lives. Once he arrives, you can find him there."

"Where does he live?"

"An apartment on Kow Wah Street. He shares it with another American, who is called Eddie West. Perhaps you know him?"

I shook my head.

"Both have been away from Hong Kong," Jimmy continued. "This Eddie West also returns today. From Rome, where, he has been for the past three weeks. His plane arrives at the airport on Kowloon in just two hours."

"Jimmy, I take it all back," I said. "I guess you are going to earn your money. Anything else?"

"A little. It is known that both Whitey Blake and Eddie West are criminals, and that they make much money this way. It is not known exactly what they do, but around the waterfront the guess is that they smuggle narcotics."

"But it might be jewelry," I said.

"Of course. It is also said that both men are killers and have killed many men. Always with a gun. It is believed that they work with several others, all Chinese."

"Anything on them?"

"So far I have been able to learn the name of only one. He is Ma Tsing, who long worked on the waterfront with various Hong Kong gangs. He was known as a skillful thief. But now he has more money than he ever did before. He left Hong Kong with Eddie West, and perhaps will return with him."

"Good work," I said. "I don't suppose you've come across anything more on the man who tried to knife me?"

He shook his head. "It is very strange. Chan Chok How bragged everywhere that he was going to make a lot of money, but I can find no one who knows who hired him."

"Could it have been part of the Blake and West gang?"

"It is possible. The Chinese who work with them probably all came from the waterfront and would have known Chan Chok How."

I was beginning to feel much better, now that there was a possibility for some sort of action. "You can do one more thing for me, Jimmy," I said. "About the time that the plane from Rome arrives, phone the airport and have Mr. West paged. When he answers the phone, you can pretend you were trying to call a different Mr. West, or any other excuse that occurs to you."

He smiled broadly. "That is so you will be able to recognize this Eddie West?"

"Right. Now, run along. I'm going to be busy. I'll probably see you later."

He nodded and was gone.

I took a shower, shaved, and got dressed. Then I went out and found a place where I could rent a car. I picked out a Jaguar and drove off, after leaving a cash deposit. It was a good thing that Robert Carlin hadn't seemed to care about keeping the expenses down.

I killed some time, then drove over and parked the car near the Kowloon ferry pier. I took the ferry across and went to the air terminal. I sat down to wait. The plane was only ten minutes late. They'd been paging Mr. West over the loudspeaker for twelve minutes by the time the passengers began filing in from the plane. I watched carefully. The man who responded was as typical as Whitey Blake had been. He was small and dark, with sharp features and the wary manner of a man who's learned always to look for trouble. He wore expensive clothes, but they, like his features, were just a little too sharp. There was a tall, well-dressed Chinese with him. They exchanged a few words, and the American went off in the direction of the phones.

I had my man spotted, so I went out and waited by the ferry. After a while, Eddie West and the Chinese came out of the customs office and boarded the ferry. By that time I was already aboard. I noticed that Eddie West automatically checked to see if anyone was on his tail.

When the ferry pulled into its slip on the Victoria side, I was one of the first persons off. I headed straight for my car and started the motor. Eddie West was already hailing a taxi. As it pulled away with Eddie and his companion in it, I fell in behind, letting a couple of cars get between me and the taxi.

It was a pretty good guess that Eddie West would head for his apartment, and I had the address, but there was always the chance that he might make a drop somewhere first. There was no point in taking chances. We wound through the crooked, narrow streets of Hong Kong and finally arrived at Kow Wah Street. The taxi stopped in front of a modern apartment building. I drove on past and turned at the next corner. As soon as I was out of sight, I parked the Jaguar and walked back to the corner. I was just in time to see the empty cab pulling away from the front of the building.

There was a small curio store across the street from the apartment house. I went in and pretended to be looking at the wares, but I stayed where I could watch the building.

I didn't have much to go on. I was guessing that Eddie West and the Chinese might have been on a mission similar to the one that Whitey Blake had been on. If they had returned with jewelry, they would have to deliver it somewhere. They might do it right away, or they might wait until sometime later.

The owner of the curio shop was beginning to be impatient with me, when I finally saw Eddie West and the Chinese coming out of the building. I murmured my apologies to the store owner and left. I headed straight across the street, as the

Chinese hailed a taxi. I timed my walk so that I was passing them just as they got into the cab. I heard the Chinese telling the driver to take them to the Hou Te Fu on Des Voeux. I knew it was a restaurant. Of course, they might have been meeting someone there, but both men were empty-handed, so I decided to gamble that they weren't. Neither one of them paid any attention to me as I went by and entered the apartment building.

A glance at the bells in the lobby told me that Eddie West and Chester Blake had an apartment on the third floor. There was no one in the lobby, and it took me only a few minutes to pick the lock of the entry door. I went into the hallway. There were self-service elevators. I took one to the third floor. Someone passed me as I went down the hall, but he was inside the elevator by the time I reached the right apartment. The lock on it was a little harder to pick, but I had it open within two minutes. I stepped into the apartment.

It had four rooms and the musty smell of a place that has been empty for a while. The furniture was adequate, but it looked like a furnished place or a bachelor apartment. Eddie West had just dumped his suitcases down in the living room without bothering to unpack them.

I stood there, considering them for a minute. There was nothing else in sight, so I decided to look at them. I knelt on the floor and tried the first suitcase. It was locked, but it was easier to pick than the door had been. I opened it and looked carefully through the clothes. I examined the bottom to see if there was a compartment there. No luck. Then I opened the second suitcase. It seemed about the same as the other, at first glance. I went through the clothes quickly and examined the bottom. Still no luck. I turned my attention to the only thing left. It was one of those leather cases for shaving equipment. I opened it and looked through it. Nothing that wasn't supposed to be there.

I was about to put it back and give up, when it seemed to me that the case was thicker than it should be. I took another look. I removed the shaving equipment and examined the case again. Finally I found it. There was a tiny camouflaged button in one corner, and when I moved it the bottom sprang up. It was a neat little compartment, but that wasn't what made me whistle softly. It was the necklace I was looking for, two bracelets, three rings, and several individual pieces of carved white jade. I was no expert, but I didn't have to be to see that they were valuable.

I looked at them long enough to be able to describe them from memory, then pushed the false bottom back into place.

I put the shaving equipment back, pulled the zipper, and put the case where I'd found it. I was about to close the suitcase when I heard a key in the lock of the door.

There wasn't much time to do anything. I left the suitcase the way it was and moved quickly over to the wall where I'd be behind the door as it opened. Jimmy Shan hadn't mentioned any third person living here with the two men, so either Blake had come back earlier than expected, or West had forgotten something and returned for it.

The lock clicked and the door swung open. Eddie West stepped inside. Praying that he was alone, I waited until he started to turn to close the door and then made my move.

Putting all my weight behind it, I hit him right on the corner of the jaw. He grunted in surprise and pain and went staggering across the floor.

I didn't wait to see him fall. I glanced through the open door, knowing that if the Chinese were there, I'd have to move even faster. But the hall was empty. I swung the door shut and whirled back to Eddie West. He'd already fallen. One leg was twitching, then he suddenly relaxed with a sigh. He was unconscious, and ought to stay that way for three or four minutes.

I opened the door and stepped into the hallway. There was no one in sight. I didn't bother with the elevator, but went down the stairs as fast as I could, not slowing up until I hit the lobby. Sure enough, there was a cab waiting in front of the building and the Chinese was sitting in it. I walked casually past it, crossed the street, and went on down to the corner. As soon as I was around it, I hurried to my car. A moment later I pulled away from the curb and headed for the hotel. I took my first deep breath then.

I made it back to the hotel without anything happening. Not that I expected it to. Eddie West had never caught a glimpse of me, and the Chinese hadn't taken a good enough look to remember much of a description. But in the meantime they were tipped off. The fact that the suitcase was still open would mean only one thing to them—although they might hope that I hadn't found the jewelry. And once Whitey Blake returned, or as soon as they reported to their friends, whoever they were, they'd know who had been in the apartment. I'd been getting plenty of attention—now I'd probably get more.

Back at the hotel, I went to my room, poured myself a healthy shot of V.O., and got on the phone to Frank Burney's office. He was in.

"I haven't picked up anything since I talked to you this morning," he said when he came on. He sounded as if he might be feeling a little pressured.

"I didn't call to ask," I said. I gave him the address on Kow Wah Street. "That's where Whitey Blake is living. With another hood named Eddie West. Which brings me to the point of this call. I want you to put a stakeout on this Eddie West. Make it twenty-four hours a day. I want to know everything he does and everyone he sees. Better put someone on Blake the same way."

"That'll mean hiring four extra men," he said.

"So hire them. A couple or three days will probably be all that we need anyway. Get them started on West as soon as you can. Now, there's something else I want you to do."

"What?"

"Ever hear of Hsu Chin Kwang?"

"Sure, I've heard of him. He's one of the wealthiest men in Hong Kong. What about him?"

"I want you to dig up everything you can on him. I don't give a damn how wealthy he is. I'm pretty certain that all that jewelry I'm after is coming into Hong Kong. It has to go someplace once it gets here."

"You mean you think he's back of it?" Burney sounded shocked.

"Somebody has to be. And nobody is selling the jade that's stolen. Hsu Chin Kwang collects jade. So get what you can for me."

"I'll do what I can," he said. "And I'll get the extra men right away. I—I may need some extra expense money."

"I'll drop it off at your office this afternoon, so that we don't lose any time."

"Well, I'll say one thing for you, March," he said. "You seem to make things hop. You've already found out more than I have, and you're a stranger in town."

"Maybe that's the reason," I told him. "I want to get it over with and go back where I came from. I'll talk to you." I hung up, waited a couple of minutes, and then picked up the phone again. I asked them to send up a bellboy with some ice and cablegram blanks. The boy arrived quickly—word must have spread that I was generous with money. I tipped him and sent him on his way. I made another drink, this time with ice, and settled down to writing a cablegram to Robert Carlin. It went something like this:

FIND OUT IF ANYTHING VANISHED FROM EUROPE IN LAST THREE WEEKS. TRY ROME FIRST. A NECKLACE, TWO BRACELETS, THREE RINGS, AND SEVERAL INDIVIDUAL UNSET PIECES. ALL WHITE JADE COVERED WITH HAND-CARVED CHARACTERS. CABLE ANSWER AND ALSO MORE EXPENSE MONEY. SEND AT ONCE VIA AIR MAIL A COMPLETE LIST AND DESCRIPTION OF ALL MISSING STUFF. THE ACTION IS LOOKING UP BUT DON'T KNOW WHO IS WINNING YET.
MILO MARCH

I had the bellboy sent back up and gave him the message with instructions to be sure that it was sent off at once. I gave him enough money to ensure complete obedience. He left the room on the run.

I had thought that I might go out and watch Whitey Blake arrive, but there wasn't any point to it. He'd certainly recognize me if he saw me, and it might lead to a showdown before we learned anything. It would be better to let Burney's men follow him and see what we could pick up.

I drove the Jaguar down to Frank Burney's office and dropped off some money for him. He wasn't in, but I talked to Linda for a few minutes. I didn't tell her what I was doing that night, but did tell her that I was busy. I said I'd call her if I got through early, otherwise I'd be in touch with her the next day. She said fine and we left it at that. I went back to the hotel and relaxed until it was time to go pick up Mei Hsu.

I drove up into the hills and parked in the driveway of the house. I went up to the front door, and the same houseboy let me in and led me to the room where I'd waited the day before. It was about five minutes before she made her entrance. And I do mean entrance. She was even more beautiful than I remembered her from the day before. She was wearing the same sort of Chinese dress, with high collar and slit skirt. It's probably about as sexy a dress as a woman can wear, and she filled it in just the right places.

"You approve of the way I look?" she asked. She knew damn well I did, for the tone of her voice was one of pleasure.

"That's one way of putting it," I said. I remembered our conversation of the day before. "I approve—but does your father?"

She laughed. "Of course not. My father believes that women should still dress as did my ancestors, in jacket and pants, and should not invite themselves to be taken out by strange men."

"I'm not a strange man," I protested. "I've met your father and I've seen you twice. That practically makes me an old friend of the family."

"My father might think differently. Shall we go, Milo? It is all right if I call you Milo?"

"Call me anything else and I won't know who you're talking to," I said. "We shall go."

We went out and got into the Jaguar. I backed out into the street. "Which way?" I asked.

"Go down to Bonham Road and turn left." I looked a question as I started down the hill.

"You know our food," she said, "but I think I can still give you a pleasant surprise. We are going to Aberdeen."

That didn't mean anything to me, but I said nothing. Within a few blocks we hit Bonham Road and I turned left.

"Stay on this road until just past the university, when you will come to Pokfulam Road, then turn left again."

"Okay," I said. I glanced at her. She was staring straight ahead, and her face was soft and warm. "You speak English with an American accent rather than British. You must have spent some time in America."

"I went to school there. Smith College."

I laughed and she looked at me curiously. "I was just thinking," I said, "that I never thought I'd have to travel this far to go out with a Smith girl. How come your father sent you there?"

"Oh, he didn't approve," she said with a smile. "But I insisted on going to college, and I refused to marry the nice young man he had picked out for me, and finally there wasn't much else he could do. My father is an intelligent man, and after two wives and several dozen concubines, he has learned that there comes a time when you can no longer argue with a woman. As a matter of fact, since then he has seldom tried."

"A wise man," I murmured.

We soon reached Pokfulam Road and I turned left. We began the winding route that led across the island to the other side. We were quickly away from the atmosphere of the city, and began to pass the squatter settlements with their little huts and cattle pens tucked between the hills. It was a pleasant ride and there were not many cars on the road. There was one far ahead of us and a small European car was some distance behind us. Finally, we were coming down into Aberdeen.

"Have you ever heard of Tien Hou?" she asked.

"Certainly," I said. "The Queen of Heaven, and also the Queen of the Sea who protects fishermen."

She looked surprised. "There's a temple to her here. There are very few of them around now—especially since I'm sure they have all been destroyed on the mainland."

"Probably," I admitted. "I just hope they have left a few kitchen gods around. I've always liked the idea of smearing his lips with honey and giving him a feast once a year, so that he will report only good things to the Overlord of Heaven about the humans in his care. It seems such a pleasant and harmless form of bribery and such a charming god to accept it."

She laughed. "I never heard one of the old gods defended in such a flattering manner," she said. "And do you think you have to resort to bribery in order to ensure a good report to heaven at the end of the year?"

"It's best to play safe," I said. "Especially with the thoughts I get when I look at you."

She laughed again, but didn't answer.

Following her directions, I drove until we came to the waterfront. I parked the car and we walked to where there were dozens and dozens of Chinese boats, each operated by an old woman in the traditional pants and jacket, wearing aprons and round straw hats. Farther out, beyond them, I could see a number of larger boats, some of them with Chinese characters in neon lights on them.

As soon as they saw us, the women from the smaller boats crowded around us, shouting at us. Some even looked as if they would grab us and pull us into their boats. Mei Hsu coolly chose one woman and indicated that we would use her boat. Smiling triumphantly, the old woman led the way to her boat.

"What's this?" I asked as we climbed into the boat. "A sea voyage to improve our appetites?"

"We are going out there," Mei said, gesturing toward the larger boats. "Those are the floating restaurants of Aberdeen. You will see that it is worth the trip."

The sampan soon reached one of the large boats and maneuvered so that we could climb aboard.

"How much should I pay her?" I asked Mei.

"Nothing now," she said. "She will wait until we are ready to return. She will receive any food that is left over from our dinner, and you will pay her for her time. Come."

We clambered aboard the floating restaurant and I looked around. It was quite a sight. First there was the main boat, which looked as if it might once have been used for fishing, but now it was clean and gay, with tables and chairs and hundreds of Chinese lanterns. Many of the tables were already filled. There were a few Westerners, but most of the customers were Chinese. Many of these were playing mahjong at their tables as they waited for food.

At right angles to the boat, a sort of floating platform was secured, which was lit with hurricane lamps. On it there was a whole row of cooks and assistants preparing food.

Alongside the boat there were tanks filled with live fish and seafood of all sorts. A man in a small boat moved from tank to tank and fished out specimens to be examined and accepted or rejected by diners.

A man appeared, seemed to recognize Mei, and steered us to a table.

"First we will have a drink," she said. "There are no cocktails here, but we can start with either wine or whiskey. The whiskey is all Chinese, I'm afraid. But if you like strong whiskey, you will like it."

"I'll try the whiskey," I said. "What do you suggest?"

"Well, they have Mui Gwai Lo, Ng Gar Pai, Sam Ching, and Lor Mai Tsao. The last one is, I think, the best."

"Then we'll have it," I said. I nodded to the waiter who had been standing by and listening.

He hurried off and was soon back with two glasses and a squat bottle. He poured drinks for us and left, leaving the bottle on the table. I tried mine. She was right. It was strong, but good.

We had three or four drinks, and then went to see about

ordering our food. We stood at the railing and watched as the man below fished out lobsters and squid and shrimp, then red-spotted garoupas, blue-banded lentjans, silvery pomfrets, and green wrasses. At Mei's suggestion, we chose giant shrimp, two huge lobsters, and a pomfret. We watched while the man below tossed our choices onto the platform, where a boy with a net caught them and passed them along to the cooks. Then we went back to our table.

The waiter had brought hot tea and watermelon seeds while we were gone. We both passed up the tea for more whiskey, but we did crack the melon seeds and eat them. Finally the food was brought.

She'd been right. It was memorable food—especially the lobster, which was cooked in a red sauce with brown sugar and red peppers. But the shrimp and the steamed fish ran a close second, and along with the food we had a wonderful hot yellow wine. Long before we were anywhere near to finishing the mounds of food, I was a contented man.

After dinner, we lingered over tea and assorted sweets and talked idly. She was an intelligent woman as well as a beautiful one, and I enjoyed myself. What more can a man ask than a wonderful meal, a beautiful woman, and interesting conversation?

Then we left. The woman was still waiting in her sampan beside the boat. We climbed down, and she rowed us back to shore, where I paid her. Then we made our way through the throng of women. We walked along the dock in the direction of the parked car.

We had gone only a few feet when suddenly something

smashed into me from behind, sending me sprawling to the ground. As I hit, I heard a thud near me.

Lying flat on the boards, I looked up. Directly in front of me there was a wharf post. A long-bladed knife was sticking in it, the handle still quivering.

FIVE

Only a few seconds went by while I lay there staring at a knife which I knew had been meant for me. The dock had suddenly grown quiet. I could hear the startled breathing of Mei Hsu and farther off the sound of running feet. I pushed against the boards and got to my feet, turning around.

There was a figure running away in the distance, but my attention was caught more by the man who stood right behind me. He was obviously the one who had knocked me down. It was Jimmy Shan.

"What the—" I began.

"So sorry," he interrupted, and to my surprise he seemed to have lost his perfect English. He was speaking almost a pidgin English. "This most awkward person stumbled over own feet to the shame of my ancestors. So sorry." And he turned, and bolted in the same direction the fleeing man had taken.

"Milo!" Mei exclaimed, putting her hand on my arm. "Are you all right?"

"I seem to be," I said, "with the exception of a bruised ego and slightly dusty clothes." I brushed off the latter, then looked up at her. "Did you see what happened?"

"Not much," she said. "I heard someone behind us, but didn't look around until you were knocked down and that knife hit the post. Then I looked, and saw the man who

bumped into you and another man near him who was starting to run. I didn't pay much attention. I was more concerned
about you."

The boat women were beginning to crowd around and
others were coming down the docks. "Come on," I said. "We
can talk on the way to the car. … Did you see the man who
first started to run?"

"Yes. But I don't remember what he looked like. He was
Chinese. I think he was dressed as if he might be a dock-
worker. I got a better look at the other man, the one who
knocked you down. When you first looked at him, I thought
you knew him. Did you?"

"No," I said. There was no way of knowing who might over-
hear our conversation, and for some reason Jimmy Shan had
wanted to act as if he and I were strangers. I didn't know why,
but I'd play along. If he hadn't knocked me down, I might
have been dead. "I think I was just surprised that he was
standing there. I guess I thought that he was attacking me."

"He probably saved your life," she said. "That knife was
thrown at you, wasn't it?"

"It looked that way," I admitted.

We reached the car and got in, and I started the motor. We
left there in a hurry.

"But why?" she asked when we were under way. "It seems
impossible that anyone would deliberately try to kill you."

"You can be sure it was no accident," I said. I laughed.
"Honey, you're in the unique position of being able to do a
new version of one of our oldest jokes. Tomorrow, if anyone
asks you who was that Occidental they saw you with last

night, you can answer, 'That was no accident, it was assault with intent to kill.' "

"How can you joke at a time like this?" she asked. "And with such a terrible pun, too. Does this have anything to do with the stolen jade you talked about with my father?"

"It might," I admitted.

"But that must mean you are close to finding who stole it?"

"If I am, it's the best-kept secret in the world, for even I don't know about it."

"But why else would they try to kill you?"

"Maybe to keep me from getting close—since I seem to have come farther than anyone else."

"Are you going to the police?" she asked.

"Not me," I said. "I'm no gossip. I started out on a date with a beautiful woman, and I intend to continue."

This time we stayed on Pokfulam Road until it hit Queens Road, and then took that into the heart of the city. We went to the Gripps nightclub in the Hong Kong Hotel. We had some more to drink and we danced. She was as light as a bamboo reed in my arms, and her head on my shoulder made the whole evening worthwhile—even the knife throwing.

It was about midnight when we left the nightclub and got into the Jaguar.

"It's a fine night for a drive up into the hills," I said as we started.

"It would be," she said, "but that's not where we are going."

"Oh? Where, then?"

"I have an apartment down in the city, and when I'm out late I stay there so as not to disturb the household."

"A separate apartment? Your father "

"… doesn't approve," she finished with a laugh. "Nevertheless, I have an apartment."

She did, too. When we got there, she invited me up for a final drink of Lor Mai Tsao. The apartment looked to be seven or eight rooms, and was furnished in what seemed to be modern Chinese style. It must have cost her father a pretty penny.

She put me on a low silk couch and went to a teakwood bar. She came back with the two drinks and sat close beside me. We had been talking all evening, but suddenly the conversation seemed to come to a stop. We didn't drink much either. After the second sip I put my glass down and looked at her. She carefully set her glass on the table beside her, and a moment later was in my embrace. A couple of minutes later I stood up, picked her up in my arms, and with her giving me directions, carried her into the bedroom.

"I wonder if your father would approve," I said, and smothered her soft laughter with my mouth.

It was sometime later that I carried our two drinks into the bedroom and lit a couple of cigarettes. I lay there, smoking and drinking and admiring her body. It, too, was like something carved out of pale jade. And we talked again easy, relaxed talk that wasn't meant to say anything. After a while, when she was getting sleepy, I got up and dressed. I kissed her gently on the lips, promised to call her the next day, and left.

It was three o'clock when I got back to the hotel. I expected to find Jimmy Shan waiting for me, but he wasn't. For once

I was disappointed at not seeing him. I went upstairs, left a call for nine the next morning, and went to sleep.

The telephone pulled me out of a deep sleep. It was the girl telling me that it was nine o'clock. I thanked her and asked her to connect me with room service. I asked them to send me up some bacon and eggs, coffee, and ice cubes. I put the phone down, lit a cigarette, and concentrated on staying awake. I was slightly hung over and I hadn't had enough sleep.

The waiter arrived with a table and pushed it over next to the bed. I signed the check, adding the tip, and he left. I poured myself a generous portion of V.O., added a couple of ice cubes, and sloshed it around to cool the whiskey. I finished it in two gulps and began to be conscious again.

When I finally felt strong enough to give some attention to the eggs, I noticed there was an envelope on the table beside the plate. It was a cablegram. Inside, there was a check and a message. The check was for three thousand dollars. The message read:

JADE OF THAT DESCRIPTION STOLEN IN ROME TWO WEEKS AGO. BELIEVED TO HAVE BEEN TAKEN BY MAN POSING AS AMERICAN TOURIST NAMED EAST. SUSPECT VANISHED COMPLETELY. JADE INSURED FOR TWO HUNDRED THOUSAND, MEMBER COMPANY. COMPLETE LIST FOLLOWS IMMEDIATELY. LET ME KNOW IF YOU NEED MORE EXPENSES.

ROBERT CARLIN

Robert Carlin was a fine man. The check and that last

sentence convinced me of that. It even gave me an appetite. I polished off the eggs and bacon and poured a cup of coffee. While I was drinking that, I called Frank Burney.

"I just went through the reports," he said. "West was picked up at about four o'clock yesterday afternoon. He stayed in his apartment until six and then left alone. He picked up an English girl who works for an exporting company and took her to dinner at the Metropole. Afterwards, they went to Luna Park and danced until about eleven. He took the girl home to her apartment and stayed until one. He then returned to his own apartment and remained there for the rest of the night."

"He didn't meet anyone else?" I asked. "Maybe while he was with the girl?"

"Not according to the report. My man watched especially for anything like that. Now, as to Blake, we picked him up as soon as he arrived at his apartment from the airport. He left again alone at seven and went to the Hou Te Fu restaurant, where he had dinner by himself. After that he went down to the Chinese section and played fan-tan until two o'clock this morning, when he returned to the apartment. He lost a little more than five hundred Hong Kong dollars in the fan-tan game. Incidentally, my operator had to play in the game in order to continue watching Blake, and he lost two hundred Hong Kong dollars. It'll be on the expense account."

"I'm sure it will be," I observed. "Didn't Blake contact anyone either?"

"Not a soul. The other players in the game seemed to know Blake, according to the report, but no conversation went on except what you'd expect."

"Just two normal guys out for the evening," I said. "Well, keep the tails on them. Something may turn up. Anything on Hsu Chin Kwang yet?"

"I should have the complete report on him before the day is over."

"Good. Have that one typed up for me, instead of giving it to me over the phone. I want to be able to go over it carefully."

"All right. It should be ready by late afternoon."

"I'll check with you," I said, and hung up. I'd barely put the phone down when there was a knock on the door.

"Come in," I called.

The door opened. It was Jimmy Shan, looking as dapper as ever. He carried a morning newspaper under his arm and might have been a Chinese commuter on his way to the office.

"It's about time," I said. "When I don't particularly want to see you, you're here every time I turn around. When I do want to see you, it's another matter."

"I'm sorry," he said. "I'm afraid that I was rather busy last night until quite late."

"Which reminds me," I said, "what was the idea of that act last night in Aberdeen? And how come you were there so conveniently?" I noticed he was looking at the bottle of V.O. "Help yourself to a drink. Maybe it'll loosen your tongue a little."

He went to the bathroom and came back with a glass. He put in some ice cubes and splashed in the whiskey.

"Well," he said, "to tell the truth, I was there because I'd been following you. I've been doing it quite often since you hired me."

"Why? I'm only paying you ten dollars a day, and you said that you had other jobs."

"It occurred to me that you are perhaps working on a very important and dangerous mission—and it would seem that I was right. So it also occurred to me that if I were helpful, you might think of rewarding me in some way at the end of the job."

"Well, you're honest," I said. "Let's get back to last night. You were following me. Was it you in that small European car I noticed behind me as I drove through Pokfulam Gap?" He nodded.

"You followed us to Aberdeen," I continued. "Then you must have waited on the dock all the time we were on the floating restaurant?"

"Yes," he said. "But it was time well spent. I had already spotted the man who later tried to kill you. I didn't know who he was, but knew that I had seen him around the waterfront in Hong Kong. So when you and the young lady returned, I followed close behind you and watched him. When he started to throw the knife, I was ready to act. I am sorry that it was necessary to knock you to the ground."

"I'll overlook it under the circumstances," I said. "But what was that act that you put on about shaming your ancestors?"

He smiled broadly. "Pretty good, wasn't it? There were many people there on the dock, and among them there might have been one or more who would carry the story for payment. I thought it was better not to expose myself more than necessary. Those are very rough people who are after you."

"Uh-huh. And if you were going to chase after the guy who threw the knife, why did you wait until I got up and turned around?"

"I thought you might recognize me even if I were running away. So I stayed in order to warn you not to reveal that you knew me. Otherwise, you might have called my name."

"All right," I said. "Let's move on to more important things. Did you catch the guy?"

"No. Unfortunately, he was very fast. But it did him no good. It was only a matter of time after I returned to Hong Kong before I learned who he was."

"Who?"

"His name is Thomas Luk. He is known as a very bad man with a knife. He came here several years ago from your country—San Francisco, I believe—because he was wanted for murder there. Since then he has worked with many different groups on the waterfront."

"For Po Hing?"

"Once, but not for several years."

"But I don't suppose you could find out who hired him?"

"Oh, yes. He was hired by the other man you are interested in. Whitey Blake."

"How did you find out?"

"I asked Thomas Luk," he said.

"And he told you just like that?" I asked.

"Yes. I believe that it may have helped that I was holding a knife at his throat when I asked. It was a very sharp knife."

I stared at him in amazement. "And you were afraid of being recognized in Aberdeen?"

"This is different," he explained. "It is true that Thomas Luk may hold some grudge against me for a while, and I will have to watch out for that, but he will tell no one that he gave me information. He will not want to be known as one who talks about his employers, and he will not want anyone to know that I held a knife at his throat. So it will be a matter between Thomas Luk and myself."

"I see," I said. "Well, I probably owe you a lot more, but let's start off by saying that beginning with yesterday your salary is doubled."

"That will be satisfactory," he said. "But if there is a reward at the end of the case, I will not refuse it."

"Good of you," I said. "Will I see you later?"

"Of course," he said, but he didn't get up from the chair. "Do I understand that you are interested in all stolen jade?"

"Most of it," I said. "Why?"

"Have you seen this morning's paper?"

"Not yet. What's happened?"

"It is a habit which has its advantages," he said solemnly. "There is an old proverb in my country which says, 'Man who does not listen to the world each morning may not even hear the cock crow.' "

"And there is an old proverb in my country," I said, "which I just wrote, that says, 'Man who does not answer questions may get a poke in the nose.' "

He gave me that beaming smile again. "Clever, these Occidentals," he said. "Sometime last night the home of Hsu Chin Kwang was broken into and many valuable pieces of jade taken. The police promise that there will be an early arrest."

"Let me see," I said.

He tossed the folded paper to me. "There are no details as yet. You will find little more than I have told you."

He was right. It was a very short story on the front page. Hsu's houseboy had discovered that someone had broken in, when he got up early in the morning. Nobody was quite sure at press time what had been stolen. Hsu Chin Kwang was checking. The wealthy collector's daughter had been away from home at the time. Nothing more.

"Very suspicious, the daughter being away," Jimmy Shan said gravely. "It is most fortunate that she was in the company of a man already at work on the case. It is to be trusted that her person was thoroughly searched by the man, so that he can later testify that it was not an inside job."

I threw the paper at him and he dodged, chuckling.

"Get out of here and get to work," I said. "Then maybe I can get to work, too. I'm beginning to think you're a Peeping Shan."

He finished the last of his drink and stood up. "I will see you later, March *hsien.*"

"Call me Milo," I said, "only get the hell out of here."

He smiled and left. I picked up the phone and called Frank Burney again. "Are you sure," I asked, "that those reports on Blake and West are accurate?"

"Yes," he said. "The men who made them have worked for me often and have always been very responsible. Why do you ask?"

"Hsu Chin Kwang was robbed last night."

There was a moment of silence. "I haven't seen a paper

yet," he said. "I usually get one on the way to the office, but I didn't stop this morning, because I was late."

"I didn't see one either," I said, "until someone just brought it to me. A fine pair of detectives we are. But West or Blake, if not both of them, must have been involved in the robbery."

"I will vouch for the men I put on this job," he said firmly.

"All right, you should know. But make sure they're on the job now. And don't forget to have that report to me this afternoon. I think there's something funny about this. Hsu hasn't been robbed in all these years, and now, when I'm beginning to get suspicious of him, he is suddenly a victim. I don't believe in coincidences. ... I'll talk to you later."

I hung up and thought a minute. Then I put in a call to Mei Hsu at her apartment. I had taken the number the night before. She answered sleepily on the fourth ring.

"Good morning," I said. "This is Milo."

"Good morning, darling," she said. "Does this mean that you're missing me already?"

"Not quite," I said. "Sorry to be so abrupt, but I'll whisper sweet nothings into your ear some other time. Your father was robbed last night and I thought you ought to know."

"My father ... ? Is he all right?"

"I think so. All I know is what was in this morning's paper. Apparently someone broke in last night and walked off with some of his jade. The story also mentioned that you were away at the time. I'm surprised that the police haven't already phoned you."

"My father wouldn't tell them where I am," she said. "He would consider it shameful that his daughter was in any house other than his. I'd better get there as fast as I can. Thanks, Milo, for telling me."

"Just part of the service," I said.

"The parts I've seen so far are wonderful," she said. "Call me."

I promised I would and hung up. Then I called the Hong Kong police. I said that I wanted to talk to whoever was in charge of the robbery of Hsu Chin Kwang. After considerable delay and being switched to two or three different persons, I ended up with a sergeant who informed me that Inspector Hemming was at Hsu's house and asked what the nature of my call was. I told him it was friendly and hung up.

After a fast shower, I shaved and got dressed and went downstairs. I got the Jaguar from the hotel garage and drove up into the hills as fast as I could. There were a couple of strange cars in the driveway, so I knew I must be in time. I parked in front of the house and went up to the door. In answer to my ring, it was opened by a Chinese constable.

"Is Inspector Hemming here?" I asked.

"He's busy," he said. "What's this about?"

"Tell the Inspector that it's about the robbery here. I'm a representative of an American insurance association."

"Wait here," he said. He closed the door in my face and I waited. When the door was finally opened again, there was a different man there. This one was older, obviously British, but with an expression on his face that made me like him at once. He was wearing a blue serge suit.

"I'm Inspector Hemming," he said. "The constable said that you wished to see me about the robbery."

"Yes," I said. "My name is Milo March. I'm in Hong Kong representing the Personal and Inland Marine Insurance Association of America. I am particularly interested in thefts of jade—as a matter of fact, I was here the night before last, speaking to Hsu Chin Kwang about the subject."

"Won't you come in?" He stood aside so that I could step into the hallway. But he made no move to leave the spot just inside the door.

"Did your company have insurance on Mr. Hsu's jade?" he asked.

"I don't know," I said. "The Association represents a great many insurance companies, with branches and connections all over the world. Recently there have been many thefts of jade in different countries, and we believe they are all connected. We also believe that in some way Hong Kong plays an important part in the picture."

"I see," he said. "How long have you been in Hong Kong, Mr. March?"

"This is my fourth day."

"You of course checked with the police when you arrived?"

"Of course," I said, with my most innocent look. "I spoke to an Inspector Simmons at the Central Police Station. We pledged mutual cooperation."

"Oh? How has that been working out?"

"Not too good. I haven't really had anything to cooperate about. When I do, I will naturally turn to the police. I haven't heard from the Inspector either—but perhaps for the same reason."

"Perhaps," he said. "What did you want here, Mr. March?"

"Some of that mutual cooperation," I said with a smile. "I'd like to know what's going on, and I'd like the opportunity to keep abreast with the case as it develops. That's all."

"I see," he said, but it was impossible to tell whether he believed me or not. "Well, there isn't much at the moment. We've only been on the case for about two hours. The house was broken into sometime last night. Entry was made through a window, and our examination convinces us it was done by an expert. No one in the house was disturbed. At the moment it is our belief that the thief knew exactly what he was looking for, as there was no evidence of ransacking. I believe that about covers it up to the moment."

"No fingerprints?"

"None, except for those who are in residence here."

"Do you know what's missing yet?"

"Mr. Hsu just completed an inventory, but I have not yet had the opportunity to go over it carefully."

"The paper mentioned that you expected an early arrest."

He permitted himself a brief smile. "We do, but as yet we do not know who it is we expect to arrest."

"May I see Hsu Chin Kwang for a moment?"

He considered it. "I don't see why not—if Mr. Hsu doesn't object. Come on."

I followed him down the hall to the room where I'd had tea the first time.

"Wait here," he said. "I'll ask if he wishes to see you." He went through the door and I waited.

A moment later he looked out. "He'll see you. But don't stay long. We have to get on with it."

I went in. The old man was sitting in about the same position as when I'd last seen him.

"March *hsien*," he said in Chinese, "my house is honored by your visit."

"I am most fortunate," I replied in the same language, "to be shown into the presence of Hsu Chin Kwang. I have been in sorrow since learning of your loss last night."

"It is nothing," he said.

"Did the thieves take much?" I asked.

"No more than ten pieces, all from the Ch'en dynasty. They were not my most valuable pieces, although they were pleasing to the eye."

"Were they insured?"

"Oh, yes. Money will be paid, but the pieces cannot be replaced."

"I know," I said. "It is a great tragedy."

"One which the world will survive," he said with humor. "It is only important that I still have my *han yu,* which can return to its origins with me."

"If there is any way in which I can be of assistance," I said, "I will be honored to do so."

"It is I who am honored," he said.

I returned his bow, backing toward the door. "May Kuan Yin once more smile on you."

I left, and the Inspector followed me out into the hallway. "Where'd you learn to speak the language like that?" he asked.

"There was a war, remember? Somebody in Washington had the bright idea of sending me to China."

"Did you learn anything from him?"

"Nothing that you haven't or won't, I'm sure. Most of our conversation was over which one of us was being honored. Where are you stationed, Inspector? I may drop in on you later."

"Police headquarters near Fenwick Pier," he said. He turned and went back into the room.

I went on down the hall. I was almost to the door when I heard my name whispered. I looked around. It was Mei. She was in the room where I'd first met her, beckoning me to come in. I went, and she closed the door.

"How is my father?" she asked.

"He seems fine," I said. "He says that only about ten pieces were taken, and they were not the most valuable."

"Was anything said about me?"

"Not a word—by your father or the police. I'm surprised the constable didn't announce that you'd come in."

"He didn't see me," she said. "I came in a side entrance, and there is no constable there."

"What are you going to tell them?"

She giggled. "That I was restless last night and went to sleep in the small apartment over our garage and just woke up. I have done that sometimes, so my father will believe it because he wants to."

"The police may not. Especially if they go to look at the apartment."

"That will be taken care of. We have an old servant who practically raised me. She doesn't like foreign white devils or police in general. She is now busy mussing up the bed in the apartment and scattering some of my clothes around.

Later, she will swear that she found me there still asleep only a little while ago."

"You sound much too efficient," I said. "Well, good luck with your story. But it's not too serious. I can always alibi you, if it is necessary."

"Not with all the details," she said. "My father "

"... wouldn't approve," I finished for her.

She laughed and kissed me lightly, and I left. The constable was still by the front door. He let me out. I got into the Jaguar and drove away.

I went back to the hotel and put the car in the garage, before walking to the bank, where I cashed the check I'd gotten, converting it into Hong Kong dollars. It made the three thousand look bigger. I returned to the hotel, put most of the money in the safe there, and went into the dining room. I had a couple of martinis and then some lunch. Finally, I went upstairs.

I made myself comfortable on the bed, picked up the phone, and called Burney's office. When the girl answered, I asked for Linda McKay. She came on a minute later.

"I'm sorry I've been neglecting you," I said, "but I've been sort of busy."

"So I heard," she said. "Frank thinks you're a real slave driver, but I think he enjoys it."

"There was a robbery in Hong Kong last night."

"I know. I read the paper. Incidentally, Frank has me working on that report on Hsu Chin Kwang for you. It'll be ready in about three hours."

"Good," I said. "Look, honey, I don't know what the schedule is going to be, but if I get a chance I'll call you tonight."

"I'll be around," she said.

I said good-bye and hung up, then thought about the case. I didn't have too much. I knew that a jade necklace had been stolen in New York and probably brought to Hong Kong. I knew that shortly after I had made a reservation to fly to Hong Kong, Whitey Blake had tried to kill me, so he was part of it. I knew that some jade jewelry had been stolen in Rome and had been brought to Hong Kong by Eddie West. I knew that a Chinese named Ma Tsing was probably also mixed up in the Rome theft. I knew that a Chinese named Chan Chok How had been hired by someone to kill me, and had in turn been killed when he failed. And I knew another Chinese named Thomas Luk had been hired by Whitey Blake to kill me. So obviously I knew too much—though it seemed little enough to me.

So much for what I knew. Then there were my guesses. I was pretty sure that Whitey Blake and Eddie West were only hired hands. The same went for Ma Tsing and the elusive Mary Moy, who had come to Hong Kong from New York. The problem was to find who was back of what was a well-organized ring, operating all over the world. Po Hing was still in the running, but my real guess was Hsu Chin Kwang. He was a collector of jade, and collectors had been known before to turn to crime to get things they couldn't buy. He had the money to start the sort of organization that was needed. He had never been robbed himself, until after I had become suspicious of him. And even then he had not been robbed of his more important pieces. I thought he was a pretty good guess, but when I got the report on him, I'd have a better idea of how well he fit into the picture.

My thoughts were interrupted by a knock on the door. Thinking it was Jimmy Shan, I called out for him to come in. The door opened and a strange Chinese stood there. He was a big one, all of six feet three or four. He was well dressed but looked about as mean as they come.

"You are the one who is called Milo March?" he asked in Chinese.

"Shih," I admitted. "Sometimes I'm called worse names. And you are?"

"It is unimportant. You are to come with me."

"I'm comfortable here," I said. "Suppose I don't want to come with you?"

He smiled without humor. "Then I make you come."

"I see," I said. "Is it just that I'm your type, or is there someone else who wants to see me?"

"Po Hing," he said. "He tells me to come and bring the foreigner known as Milo March. If he comes willingly, then I am to be nice. If not, I am to do what is necessary. Is it clear?"

SIX

It was clear enough. Not only did he look big enough to do what he was threatening, he looked as if he'd enjoy it. And my gun was still over in the dresser drawer. I was getting a little tired of all the people who seemed to be gunning for me. After this, maybe I'd wear the gun, permit or no permit.

"It's clear," I said. "It's so clear I can see the mud at the bottom. And I'm not even sure you can do what is necessary if I refuse to come with you."

"It can be arranged for you to learn."

"Where are you supposed to take me? Po Hing's house?"

"Yes."

"Well, he won't dare do much there," I said. "Let's go."

I'm not sure, but I think he looked disappointed. Still, he waited patiently for me to go ahead of him through the door. Downstairs, I suggested using my car so that no one would have to bring me back, but he insisted that I go with him. He led the way to a car that was driven by another Chinese. Once more I was on my way up into the hills. Whoever it was that said "Take to the hills, boys" didn't know how boring it could get sometimes.

We parked beside Po Hing's house and went inside, then into the same room where we'd met before. Po Hing was sitting in the same chair.

"Hi, pal," he said. He turned and told the big guy to get out. When we were alone, he turned back to me. "Help yourself to a drink."

"Maybe it's got arsenic in it," I said. "Look, I don't go much for this summons bit. If you want to talk to me, why don't you call me up and suggest that I drop around when I have the time?"

"It's quicker this way."

"I also don't like the gorilla act. The next time I may find out if your boy is as tough as he looks."

"Wing is a good man," he said amiably. "Have a drink. If it's poison, it's the best that money can buy."

"Or thieves can steal," I muttered. But I did go over to the table and pour myself a drink. When I finished, I noticed that Po Hing was still staring at me.

"I don't dig you," he said. "You're an insurance dick, right?"

"Right."

"I don't like cops, and maybe I wouldn't like insurance cops if I saw more of them. Maybe I'm starting to dislike them right now. But I figured you for a right guy when I saw you before. Now I don't know. You got any identification?"

"Tons of it," I said. I pulled out my wallet and tossed it to him. "Look for yourself."

He went through the wallet, looking at all the papers. Finally, he tossed it back to me.

"Tell me something," he said. "I don't know much about this insurance racket. I know everything about my own racket, but this is different. Maybe a guy could be an insurance dick and he's out on a case trying to find a lot of hot rocks, and at the same time he's the guy who's grabbing them in the first place. Maybe it could work like that?"

"It's been known to happen," I said, "but not with me. If that's what you have in mind, you'd better try another game where the house rules are easier."

"I don't get it," he said.

"Have you been fooling around with horse or mainlining?" I asked. "It must be one of the two, for you to come up with a wing-ding like that. Or am I too young to know?"

He opened a drawer beside him and reached inside. He came out with a piece of jade about two inches long. It was carved in the form of a bird. He tossed it on the table.

"That's what I've been smoking," he said. "And it's been making me burn. Know what it is?"

"It looks as if it was carved out of imperial jade and it's probably pretty valuable, but that's all I know. I'm no expert."

He gave me a long, searching look. "That's all you know?"

"Sure. And why be so mysterious? The only thing I know about mysteries is that the butler did it."

He sighed and poured himself a drink. "I know everything about my own racket," he said again, "and I don't know much about this sort of stuff. But I know about this one, because it was in the papers here maybe five years ago. This once belonged to some emperor on the mainland. Five years ago it was bought by a rich man in Hong Kong for twenty-five thousand dollars—American dollars. There was a big story about it in all the papers, and I remembered. That's a lot of dough to pay for a two-inch bird."

"Who bought it?"

"Hsu Chin Kwang. His house was robbed last night."

"I know it," I said. "Where'd you get that?"

He sighed again. "Now we're coming to the part I don't get. I have a reputation in this town, March. Po Hing is a guy you don't double-cross. Those who tried it once never tried it again with anyone. The last one who tried was eight years ago. Everyone knows this, even the cops. I've been living in this house for seven years, but no one comes near it unless he's invited. ... The house of Hsu was not the only one broken into last night."

"Someone broke in here, too?"

"Yes. Into this room. I discovered it about an hour ago. They clipped the wires around one window and then jimmied it. A nice professional job. About two hours ago I found this jade bird in the drawer of my desk. You add it up."

"A frame," I said.

He nodded.

"So how do I get in the picture?" I asked.

"I told you," he said. "Nobody in this town's got the guts to try a double-cross or a frame on Po Hing. You're the only fresh blood in town. You've got your own racket, and maybe it's getting hot for you. So you pull a last job, and try to stick Po Hing with the works."

"It's logical," I said. "Maybe I'd think the same way, if I were you. But it's still strictly for the birds. And it works both ways."

"What do you mean?"

"I arrive in Hong Kong," I said, "looking for a hot operator. You're one of the hottest of operators. As soon as I arrive, a guy tries to put a hole through me with a knife. The guy can't talk because he's dead, but he used to work for Po Hing. I get a little warmer on the trail, and last night another guy tried to get me with a knife. He used to work for Po Hing. So now maybe another job is pulled; one of the pieces stolen is sacrificed so that everybody will say poor Po Hing is being framed."

"You got a case, too," he said. "Maybe you ought to give up being an insurance dick and throw in with me. Who was the guy last night?"

"Thomas Luk."

"Yeah, he worked for me. A long time ago. I caught him holding out on me one night and kicked him into the river. I didn't know he could swim. Okay, we got two pictures. How do you figure them?"

"Maybe there's another smart operator in Hong Kong you don't know about," I said. "Maybe he knows that I'm getting closer than he wants me to be. He's tried to kill me three times and it hasn't worked. He needs a pigeon. Who's better than Po Hing? Everybody knows Po Hing is a smart operator, and that's what I'm looking for. Stick Po Hing with the rap and the other smart operator is in the clear."

"Who?"

"I don't know. I've got a guess, but it won't hold up yet."

"I could get Thomas Luk to talk," Po Hing said softly. "He already has. He was hired by Whitey Blake."

"Oh, yeah, the American who works with the other American. I knew they worked together, but I thought they were smuggling narcotics."

"They're in this," I said. "And there's a guy named Ma Tsing. Know him?"

"Yeah. He used to be in narcotics. He had a deal with the Reds on the mainland."

"Well, I think he's in this, too. But they're all only hired hands. Do you know anything about Hsu Chin Kwang?"

"Only that fifty years ago he was a pirate, and today he is one of the richest men on the island. You figure him in this?"

"Maybe," I said. "At this point I figure everybody—including you."

He smiled. There was a low buzzing sound in the room, and the smile vanished from his face.

"What was that?" I asked.

"The police," he said, and there was suspicion in his eyes again. "And not a routine call either." He picked up the jade figure and looked around the room.

"Give it to me," I said. "They won't be likely to search me."

He considered for only a second, then tossed the jade to me. I caught it and put it in my coat pocket. A moment later the door opened. Inspector Hemming and three other policemen came in.

"Well, Po Hing," the Inspector said, "it's been some time since I paid you a visit."

"I am always glad to see my good friends the police," Po Hing said.

"Don't think you will be this time. I have a search warrant." The Inspector looked around and saw me. "Well, Mr. March, I wasn't thinking I'd see you so soon."

"Why not?" I asked. "Po Hing and I were talking about general conditions in Hong Kong."

"I expect," Inspector Hemming said dryly. He produced a folded paper from his pocket and handed it to Po Hing. "I think you will find that in order. ... All right, men."

Two of the policemen vanished back through the door, while the third started a systematic search of the room we were in. Po Hing glanced at the paper and put it on his desk.

"What is this about, Inspector?" he asked.

"Oh, routine. We like to keep a check on you chaps, you know." He turned and followed the man who was searching the room.

Almost forty minutes went by—while Po Hing and I watched silently—before the search was over. The other two policemen returned, and shook their heads when the Inspector looked at them. Finally, it was obvious that the whole house had been gone over and nothing was found. Hemming turned to Po Hing.

"Guess you've pulled it off again," he said. "Where'd you hide it, Po Hing?"

"Hide what?" Po Hing asked blandly.

"The proceeds of the job you pulled last night."

"Last night? Inspector, I assure you that I did nothing last night that could interest you. In fact, if my memory serves me, I don't believe there are any ships unloading at the docks now."

"You know what I mean," Inspector Hemming said. He turned to me. "Mr. March, I don't suppose you'd care to tell me what you're doing here?"

"But I did tell you," I said.

"Oh yes. Well, you mentioned that we might have another

chat, Mr. March. I think perhaps this might be as good a time as any. Would you care to return to headquarters with me?"

"An arrest, Inspector?" I asked.

"Oh, no. Just a chat. Shall we go?"

I nodded, winked at Po Hing, and followed the Inspector from the room. There were two police cars outside. I got in the one with Hemming, and we started down the hill. I made a couple of attempts at conversation which got nowhere, and we finished the ride in silence. When we arrived, I followed him into his office and took the chair he indicated. A constable came in right on our heels and handed the Inspector a large manila envelope. He opened it, glanced at the contents, and placed it on his desk. Then he finally looked at me.

"Chatting about conditions, were you?" he asked pleasantly.

"Yes."

"Not about jades?"

"Not directly. But in this case, I consider the general conditions in Hong Kong very much related to the jade I'm interested in."

"To be sure," he said. "Do you know why we had a search warrant for Po Hing's house?"

"I didn't in the beginning," I said, "but I gathered from one of your remarks that you suspected him of the Hsu robbery."

"Exactly. While I was still at the house of Hsu Chin Kwang, there was a call at headquarters giving us a tip on Po Hing."

"An anonymous tip?"

"No. It came from an informer who has always been reliable. I am inclined to think that he's still reliable. Isn't that really why you were there?"

"No," I said truthfully. "I don't think that Po Hing had anything to do with the robbery."

"I see," he said coldly. "And what is your opinion of the case, Mr. March?"

"If I told you at the moment, you'd throw me out. It's that wild. But if there's anything to point to it, you can be sure that I'll get in touch with you. I promised cooperation and I'll give it."

"Will you?" he asked. He pulled the manila envelope in front of him and looked at the contents. "You may be interested to know that I spoke to Inspector Simmons after meeting you today. You may also be interested to know that we've begun to collect a considerable file under the name of Milo March."

"That's very kind of you," I murmured.

"We shall see. Let me see. You landed in Hong Kong four days ago and went to see Inspector Simmons. You explained whom you were representing, and that you were looking into the theft of considerable jade around the world. You were also looking for a Mary Moy you believed to be involved. You asked Inspector Simmons's assistance in locating this girl." He glanced up from the paper. "Incidentally, it's interesting that you haven't since checked with Inspector Simmons to see if he had any success in locating the girl."

"I assumed that he would phone me if he did," I said. "After all, we had discussed mutual cooperation."

"Exactly. Since you didn't phone, however, I can tell you

that there was no Mary Moy on any flight into Kowloon for several days during the period in which you were interested. There are many Mary Moys in Hong Kong, but none who seems to fit in with your report of events."

"Well, that's the way it goes some days," I said.

"Inspector Simmons," he continued, "as a member of Her Majesty's police force, knows that private inquiry and insurance agents quite often interfere more with the police than they help. Consequently, he thought it might be a good idea if we kept some sort of check on your activities. That explains the file."

"Very flattering," I said.

"Let me see," he said. "A number of interesting coincidences have occurred since your arrival. There was a known criminal who visited someone on your floor in the hotel and ran out later with what appeared to be a broken arm. The following morning he was found off the dock, drowned. I don't suppose it was you he visited?"

"I don't recall anyone with a broken arm," I said.

"In the meantime, you hired a private inquiry agent named Frank Burney to do certain work for you. You also became rather intimate with his partner, a Miss Linda McKay, visiting her twice in her flat. You also called on Hsu Chin Kwang and spent some time with him. The following night, which was last night, you took his daughter out and later escorted her to her apartment in the city, where you stayed until quite late."

"I didn't know you went in for that sort of thing, Inspector," I said. "If I had known, I might have brought you my collection of French postcards. They are said to be quite good."

His cheeks got a little redder, but otherwise he ignored the remark as he pored over the file. "There are three other things which I find worthy of note. Yesterday you went to the airport on Kowloon, and then followed an Eddie West to his apartment here in Hong Kong. Since then, agents who work for Frank Burney have been keeping a watch on West and another American, Whitey Blake. You have also been frequently visited at your hotel by a Jimmy Shan, who has no police record but is considered to be somewhat shady. Last night you went to Aberdeen to have dinner with the daughter of Hsu Chin Kwang. We do not know what happened there, but we do have a report which says that there was an attempt to knife a white man who was in the company of a Chinese girl. And I might add that we know today was the second time you've visited Po Hing."

He put the papers back into the envelope and carefully closed it. Then he looked up at me. "Would you care to comment on the events I have mentioned, Mr. March?"

"Sure," I said. "I believe I mentioned that I don't recall any visitor with a broken arm. I hired Frank Burney to see if he could get any information on Mary Moy. In fact, his name was one of several suggested by your Inspector Simmons. I also got Hsu Chin Kwang's name from Simmons, and I went to see him because he is presumably an expert on jade. The next point is more personal, and I must confess that I'm rather surprised by the Hong Kong police. I may even write a letter to the *Times* about it. There are only two things about me on which most people agree. I'm single and I'm male. Linda McKay and Mei Hsu are both attractive women, also single.

I don't believe in working twenty-four hours a day. So let us say that I was relaxing."

"Isn't it odd that you chose those two particular women? Miss McKay is a partner of Frank Burney's. Miss Hsu's father was robbed last night, probably while you were with her."

"You didn't mention coincidences," I said. "Shall I go on? I think you mentioned Jimmy Shan. I find him a source of much general information about Hong Kong, and amusing as well. Which brings us to Whitey Blake and Eddie West. Naturally, I don't know either man, but they are both Americans. I understand that they are considered rather shady characters. This distressed me, as it always does to find some Americans giving a bad name to all Americans in a foreign country. I hired Frank Burney to check on them in the hope that I might be able to do something to change their ways—in the interests of international good will, you understand."

"And the incident in Aberdeen last night?"

"I believe you said somebody tried to knife somebody? I suppose it's possible. At one time I noticed there was a sort of crowd around, jabbering away, but I didn't pay any attention. If there was such an attempt, I'm afraid I must have overlooked it."

"You didn't get anything the crowd was jabbering about?" he asked. "This afternoon you were speaking perfect Chinese."

"But I speak only Cantonese and Mandarin. I believe those women were using some dialect which I don't know."

"You make some very interesting explanations, Mr. March."

"I'm known for it," I said brightly. "You should see the vouchers I hand in with my expense accounts."

"No doubt," he said crisply. "There is one further thing, Mr. March. We received a routine report from the New York City police, stating that they believed a known American criminal named Whitey Blake was on his way to Hong Kong. They added that they were presently interested in him for an attempted murder of an American citizen. Would you like to know the name of that American citizen?"

"Of course. I'm always interested in my fellow citizens."

He sighed heavily. "His name was Milo March."

"Oh?" I exclaimed. "You mean that was the fellow who tried to kill me in New York? Well, what do you know? It is a small world, isn't it?"

"It is, Mr. March. And it might become considerably smaller for you unless you're careful."

"Meaning what?"

"Meaning," he said, obviously keeping his temper under control, "that the police of Hong Kong are not amused by your activities. We do not like or appreciate the efforts of amateurs like yourself, when it comes to matters of this sort. Crime is a most serious thing and is best left to those whose job it is. We are quite capable of handling the robbery of Hsu Chin Kwang and any other criminal activities which may occur here."

"I'm so glad to hear that," I said. "It does give one a sense of security to know that the police are on the job. You won't mind if I ask you one or two questions, will you?"

"Such as?"

"How long have Whitey Blake and Eddie West been in Hong Kong?"

"I believe about three years."

"How many times have they been arrested?"

"They've never been arrested," he said uncomfortably. "There has been no evidence to warrant it. I believe they have been questioned a few times, and we've kept our eye on them."

"That's very good," I said. "There's been an international ring of jewel thieves operating from here for some time. What have you done about that?"

"I don't even know that there is such a ring operating from here," he said stiffly.

"Of course, you don't. But you know almost everything about me since I've arrived here—including my sex life. That's some comedown—from Sherlock Holmes to Peeping Tom."

"Now, see here ... ," he began angrily.

"No, *you* see here," I said. "I'm a friendly guy. When I tell a cop I'm willing to cooperate, I mean it. But it doesn't mean I'm going to run to him every time I stub my toe. And it doesn't mean that I'm going to put up with being treated like a poor relative who just moved in. I don't wear a badge and I don't cost the taxpayers a cent, but I get paid for solving crimes just as you do. I get paid more than you do, and I'll bet you my next year's salary against yours that I've solved more crimes than you have."

His face was a dark red. "I could have you arrested right now for interfering with the police."

"Sure, you could. But you couldn't keep me very long. You do it, and when I get out I will make you look like a monkey. You know, I didn't ask for this little exchange. You did. And

I'm willing to stop it whenever you want to. But if you're going to try to push me around, I'm going to push right back."

He sat there, gripping his desk, and was silent for a few minutes. Slowly, the red faded from his face and his grip on the desk relaxed. He let his breath go in a long sigh.

"I suppose you're partly right," he said grudgingly. "I shouldn't have called you an amateur. But it still is highly irregular and illegal for you, or anyone other than the regular police, to try to solve crimes. You must see that."

"I didn't say I was trying to solve a crime," I said, hedging a little. "I did say that I was trying to collect information—at which I have some skill—and I said that I would turn it over to the police. I've even been so damned law-abiding that I haven't carried a gun as I usually do when I'm on a case. I'm too much of a professional to come running to you with every guess I get, and you'd throw me out if I did."

"Perhaps," he said, "but why only guesses? What about the two attacks on you?"

"If there were any attacks on me," I said with a grin, "it might have been because they didn't know whether I was guessing or not, any more than you did."

"I suppose that's possible," he said reluctantly. "Are you trying to tell me that all you will do is gather information?"

"Of course," I said. "But don't pin me too close to it. If I catch someone trying to kill me, I'm not going to relax and try to get a message to you after it's over."

"That's the trouble with you chaps," he said gloomily. "You say one thing and then go out and do something else, and claim that you couldn't help it."

"Well, there's one other solution," I said gently. "You can always go out and solve the case first. That would stop me from doing anything, even accidentally."

"Quite," he said. "All right, March. Get the hell out of here. But remember, if I catch you out of line just once, into the clink you go."

"Are you still cooperating, Inspector?" I asked.

"I suppose so," he said wearily. "We'll give you as much cooperation as we can, providing you do the same. But, naturally, we don't intend to tell you our guesses." He smiled as he said this. "Now get out so I can get some work done."

"I'll see you around," I said, and left. I patted the piece of jade in my pocket once, for luck, as I left the building. I hailed a cab and directed it to Frank Burney's office.

Burney wasn't in, but Linda was. She had the report ready for me. I told her I'd try to call her later, took it, and left. I found another taxi and went back to the hotel. This time I made sure the door was locked before I poured a drink and settled down to look at the report.

Hsu Chin Kwang was certainly a colorful character. He'd started out as a river pirate, then graduated to head of a large bandit group on the mainland. Eventually, he made a deal with the head of the Nationalist government and was forgiven all his crimes and permitted to leave. That was when he had moved to Hong Kong. It was believed, but never proven, that he hadn't changed his ways when he moved. He had started an export-import company, doing business with various countries; but the rumor had been he would get an order, then go out and steal the merchandise to fill it. Whatever the method, he grew richer and richer, finally owning a large part of Hong Kong.

The record indicated that he'd been honest, or reasonably so, for the past thirty years. But he also sounded like a man who would resort to the old methods if they were the only way he could get what he wanted. He'd always been a tough old turkey, and I was willing to bet that time had not softened him. My guess still seemed like a good one.

The phone rang. I picked it up and said hello. It was Frank Burney.

"You got the report?" he asked.

"Yeah. I stopped by and picked it up. Thanks."

"Okay. Now, I think I've stumbled across something for you. There's a little club down in the Chinese section near the waterfront. Kai Shing's. Both Blake and West go there fairly often, and I have the feeling that it's a meeting place for their gang."

"That might be something," I said. "How'd you find out about it?"

"One of my men knew about it, and then he heard Blake making plans to go there late tonight. I've decided to check on it myself. I thought you might like to go along."

"I would," I said promptly. "What time?"

"Blake made his date for one-thirty in the morning. I thought I'd get there about one. Want to meet me there?"

"Fine."

"It's on Hon Yan Road. You can't miss it. I'll see you there."

"Okay," I said, and hung up. I looked at my watch. It was almost six o'clock. I took a chance that Linda had already left the office and called her at home. She was there. I asked her if she'd like to have dinner with me. She said yes, and I told her I'd pick her up in twenty minutes. I went down, got the Jaguar, and drove over to her place. She was ready when I got there.

I drove to the Hou Te Fu on Des Voeux and we went in. We both had a couple of drinks and then ordered Peking duck.

"I have to leave you right after dinner," I told her. "I'm working with your partner tonight."

"Frank? What are you doing with him?"

"He thinks he's found a meeting place. Blake is going there tonight, so Burney and I are going to take a look."

"Where's the place?"

"Over in the Chinese section. Some place called Kai Shing's.

"Oh," she said. "Is it going to be dangerous?"

"No. We're just going to look it over."

"I know you're doing some work on your own," she said. "How is it going?"

"Pretty good, I think."

We talked about it for a while, then about other things. When dinner was over, I drove her back to her apartment. She asked me to come up, but I said no. For a minute I thought she was going to give me the "man needed—come quickly" message, but she didn't. I might have weakened if she had.

I got back to the hotel at about nine. Jimmy Shan had been there, but had left. There was no message except that he'd been there. I went upstairs, got out my gun, and made sure that it was working all right. Then I took a drink and stretched out across the bed. As soon as I finished the drink, I intended to rest until it was time to go.

That idea was stopped by the ringing of the phone. I picked it up and said hello.

"Milo," she said. There was no mistaking that voice. It belonged to Mei Hsu.

"Hello, Mei," I said. "How are you?"

"Lonely. And I'm back at the apartment."

"I have to work tonight" I said.

"When?"

"Well, I'm supposed to meet someone at one o'clock in the Chinese section."

"It's nine-thirty now," she said. "That gives you a lot of time before you're due there. Come on over."

I knew that I should rest, but I wanted to go. And that pretty well decided the matter. "All right" I said. "I'll be right over."

I hung up. I went into the bathroom and looked at myself in the mirror. I needed a shave. So while I was at it, I showered and changed clothes. I wrapped up my gun and shoulder holster in the newspaper and left the room. Law or no law, I wasn't going to be caught again without some form of self-protection.

It was only a few minutes later when I parked the Jaguar in front of her building. I put the gun and holster in the glove compartment and went upstairs. Mei opened the door for me. She was wearing a bright Oriental dressing gown, and the light behind her made it almost invisible.

She came into my arms as soon as I was in the room. There was an almost compulsive eagerness about her body. But then she pushed me away and led me to the couch where she had already poured two drinks.

"How did it go this afternoon, after I left?" I asked her.

"All right," she said. "The Inspector let me know privately that he knew where I was last night and who I was with, but I guess he considered that an alibi. My father accepted the story without question. And that's all. What happened with you?"

"Not much. I had a small brush with the Inspector myself. I accused him of being a Peeping Tom, and he didn't care much for it."

She laughed. "Let him peep. It might give him some ideas. Where are you going tonight?"

"A place called Kai Shing's."

"I've heard of it. I think it's a dangerous place. Why are you going there?"

"Work," I said briefly.

She took the hint and dropped the subject. We didn't talk much more. We finished our drinks and then, without anything being said, we got up and walked hand in hand into the bedroom.

Later we had two more drinks with our cigarettes, and finally it was time to go. She went to the door with me and I held her in my arms. She rested her head on my shoulder for a minute, then looked up and kissed me warmly. "Good-bye. Milo," she said.

"So long, honey," I said. "I'll probably call you tomorrow." I went downstairs and got into the Jaguar. I buckled on my holster and slipped the gun into it. Then I drove toward the waterfront. It took me about twenty minutes to reach the Chinese section and to find Kai Shing's. There was no place to park right beside it, but I finally found a spot a little more than two blocks away. I walked back toward the club.

Despite the lateness, everything was busy in the section. Stores were open and there were a lot of people on the sidewalk. I reached the club and glanced inside. I didn't see anything of Frank Burney and decided I'd better wait outside. But I didn't have to wait long. A taxi pulled up in front of the club and he got out. He came directly over to me.

"Sorry if I'm late," he said. "Been waiting long?"

"No more than five minutes. It looks busy tonight."

"It's always that way down here until very late at night. And you'll find more gambling on this street than Las Vegas ever dreamed about. Let's go in and find a good table."

We entered the club. It was dimly lit and fairly crowded. The air was filled with the blue haze of smoke. Burney finally picked a table over in a far corner, where it was darker. The table was also in a good position to let us see the rest of the room. Not too far from the table there was a small stage where a blonde was doing a clumsy strip while a three-piece orchestra whined along in her wake, never quite catching up.

We sat down and a waiter hovered. "I imagine the beer is safe here," Burney said. "It usually is in most of the places. But I wouldn't recommend anything." He turned to the waiter and ordered a beer. The waiter looked at me.

"Lor Mai Tsao," I said.

He looked surprised, but scurried away. He was soon back with a bottle of beer and a glass, and the glass of whiskey for me. It looked as if it contained three or four shots and there was no ice, but I decided not to fight fate. He stood waiting and Burney gave him some money.

"You usually have to pay in these places when you're served," he explained. "But don't worry. I'll put it on the expense account."

"Okay," I said. I took a sip of the whiskey. As near as I could tell, it was the real stuff.

"You're a braver man than I am," Burney said, looking at my glass. "I've never been able to go the native whiskey."

"It's not bad," I said. I looked around the room. As near as I could tell, we and the stripper were the only Westerners in the place. All of the customers were men, and none looked as if he'd ever done an honest day's work. There were mahjong games going at several tables and some sort of card game at others. "What kind of people come here?"

"I'm not sure," Burney said. "Mostly dockworkers and criminals, I imagine. I wouldn't especially want to tangle with any of them. There are probably as many knives in the room as there are people."

"The police leave them alone?"

"Pretty much. If there's a fight or anything like that, they come in and cart a bunch of them off to jail, but the rest of the time they don't pay much attention. … Here our pigeons come now."

I looked, and saw Whitey Blake and Eddie West coming in. They made their way to a table across the room where three Chinese were already sitting. I recognized one of them as the man who had been with Eddie West when he got off the plane.

"And there's my man," Burney said.

I looked at the door again and saw a small, thin-faced Chinese slip in and take a table near the door. He didn't look like much of an agent, but if he delivered the information, that was all I could ask for.

I glanced back at the table across the room. Blake and West had sat down and were ordering drinks.

"I think," Burney said, "I'll go by as if I'm stepping out for a breath of air and let him know we're here. He might even have some more information."

"Do you think that's wise?" I asked.

"They don't know me," he said. "And I think I ought to make contact with my man."

"You're running the show," I told him.

He got up and walked toward the front. I didn't bother watching him but turned back to my drink. I had just taken another sip when someone careened into my shoulder, making me spill part of the drink. I looked up, expecting to see a drunk. I was right, except that the drunk was Jimmy Shan. He was blinking down at me, weaving on his feet.

"So sorry," he said thickly. "China boy drink too much. Go home chop-chop." He staggered on back through the restaurant, bumping into other tables.

I stared after him curiously. Maybe he was drunk, but he was doing that "so sorry" act again and there must be a reason for it. Then I looked down and found the reason. There was a tiny folded piece of paper in my lap. I reached down and unfolded it. It said: *Go to the men's room in back quickly. Don't finish the drink.*

I folded the paper again and put it in my pocket. I looked around. Burney was standing by the doorway, next to the table where his agent sat, as though staring outside. I got up and threaded my way through the tables to the rear of the room. Another blonde was just starting to take her clothes off on the platform. She looked at me with unseeing eyes as I went by.

I found the men's room and went in. It was small and dirty—and empty. I had expected to find Jimmy there. Then I heard a hoarse whisper.

"Milo!"

I looked around again. There was a small open window, and framed in it was Jimmy's face. He beckoned. "Come on out this way," he said.

"Why?" I asked.

"Come out," he said urgently. "I will tell you out here." His face disappeared.

Feeling slightly foolish, I went over and climbed through the window. I found myself in a narrow, dark alley with Jimmy beside me.

"We have to get out of here," he said. "Come on." He put one hand on my arm and exerted pressure, pushing me toward the street. I went along with him.

"What's this all about, Jimmy?" I asked.

"Your drinks were drugged," he said. "The three men at the table where the two Americans went when they came in one of them is Ma Tsing. They called the waiter over and gave him instructions when they saw you enter."

"If both drinks were drugged," I said, stopping, "I'd better go back and get Burney."

"No," he said urgently. "They don't want him. They want you. They will leave him alone. If you go back, you will be killed in there."

"They wouldn't dare do that," I said, but I didn't really believe what I was saying.

"Many men have been killed in there. If you went back and they realized that you knew the drinks were drugged, they would start a fight, and in it you would be knifed. Nobody would ever know how or by whom. And the other man would be killed, too. This way you will escape and he will only have a headache tomorrow."

We went up the alley and out onto the street. It was less crowded than it had been when I arrived, but there were still quite a few people on it. The stores were still open and doing business.

"Where is your car?" he asked.

"This way," I said, pointing. "About two blocks. But I still think I shouldn't leave Burney in there."

"They will forget all about him as soon as they realize that you have left. You may yet see for yourself. We must leave. Even so, they may have left men at the car."

We walked down the street. We had gone about a block when Jimmy clutched my arm. "Look," he said. "In front of the club."

I turned and looked. There were five men standing in front of the club. Despite the distance and with the dim light, I had no trouble recognizing Whitey Blake. Even as we watched, one of the men pointed in our direction and they started walking toward us.

"You see?" Jimmy Shan said. "They are coming for you."

SEVEN

He had finally convinced me. They were coming after me, but my only reaction was one of anger. All through this case someone had been trying to use me as a clay pigeon and I was getting tired of it. I took the gun from my shoulder holster and slipped the safety catch off. Then I put it back.

"There are five of them, maybe more," Jimmy Shan said at my shoulder, "and we are only two. It would be better to continue."

He was right again. Reluctantly, I walked ahead toward the car. We had almost reached it when Jimmy stopped me. "It's as I thought," he said. "Look."

I glanced in the direction he was pointing. There was my car, and near it there were two men. "Maybe they just happen to be standing there," I said.

"No. I know one of the men, but not the other. We will go this way." He urged me toward a side street. It must have led straight to the harbor, for there was suddenly a strong smell of water as we turned into it.

There was a shout from somewhere in back of us. Glancing around, I saw that the five men were still coming and that now the two men were leaving the car and heading in our direction.

"The house has changed the odds on us, Jimmy," I said.

"It's now seven to two. Find a good place where we can stand them off, and I'll see if I can't get us better odds."

"No," he said. "I have a better idea. There is a place near here where you can hide while they go by. You give me your keys and I will slip around and get the car and come back for you."

"I don't like it," I said. "It's too much like running away."

"In China there is old proverb that says, 'Man who is too brave may not live long enough to prove it.' "

"Yeah, I know. The man who fights and runs away lives to fight another day—and all that garbage. Why are you doing all this, Jimmy? Even with your wages doubled, it hardly seems worth it."

"If you are dead, there are no wages," he said. "Besides, you have not paid me for the last day."

"Maybe I should owe you a few bucks all the time," I said. "All right, Jimmy. I'll play it your way this time, but I'm getting about ready for a payoff. Especially with that white-headed bastard."

We had reached another street and turned left into it. This one, too, had a number of shops that were open, but they seemed to be cheaper ones than those we had left. Then, directly ahead of us, I saw a curious sight. There was a man and a basket near a tall pole. The basket was bamboo and was probably about six feet in diameter and four or five feet high. The lower half of it was tightly woven, but the top half was made of interlaced bars of bamboo. There was a rope from the basket to the top of the pole and then back to the ground again. A girl or a woman was sitting inside the basket.

"What's that, Jimmy?" I asked.

"What we are looking for," he said. "Give me fifty dollars, Hong Kong money, and wait here for a minute."

I dug out fifty dollars and gave it to him. I waited while he went over and talked to the man. I couldn't hear what they were saying, but I saw the money change hands and then Jimmy came back.

"You are to get into the basket with the girl," he said, "then he will pull you up into the air, and they will not see you when they go by. They won't think of looking in the basket."

"What is this?" I asked. "I don't get it."

"The girl," he explained quickly, "is a prostitute. The man is one who you would call a pimp, and we call the horse that pulls. They cannot afford a room for the girl, so they use the basket. He pulls the girl and her customer up into the air where no one can see, and it is fine. They will never think of looking there."

It struck me funny and I began to laugh.

"There is no time," he said. "Get into the basket quickly."

Still laughing, I went over and stepped into the basket and sat down. The girl gave me an empty smile and pulled the door shut. The man began to pull on the rope and the basket began to rise.

"Milo," Jimmy called softly, "I would use it only as a hiding place. I think the girl might have the flower-and-willow sickness. And do not worry about the man. I have paid him what they would get from twenty customers. I will be right back."

I was still laughing when the basket stopped rising. All I could see was the sky and the tops of distant buildings. And looking at the bars, all I could think of was to sing "I'm only a bird in a bamboo cage."* But I didn't sing it. I looked at the girl. She was staring at me curiously. Her hands, which had started to undo her dress, had stopped. She probably thought I was mad. I wasn't sure but what she was right.

"Ni hao pu hao?" I said.

She was startled at hearing her own language from me. She ducked her head and giggled. Then she looked up at me.

"You are a strange man," she said in the same language. Her hands again got busy with the dress.

"I'm even stranger," I replied. "Don't do that. I only wish to sit here with you and tell you about the moonbeams that are caught in your hair and the stars that have come down to look from your eyes."

She giggled again and unconsciously tried to smooth her hair. In all probability, no man had ever talked to her like that—maybe no man had ever talked to her except to give an order. She was probably no more than seventeen, but she was already beginning to look old.

There was the sound of voices below. First, one in English asking if two men had run by; then the same question in Cantonese. As the man below began telling them of the two men who had passed, I suddenly remembered the purpose that this strange cage served. I moved my body around so that the cage would sway in the air.

"Tell me," I said softly to the girl, "the one below, he is your man?"

---

* "She's Only a Bird in a Gilded Cage" was a popular song of 1900. Milo would know it because Bing Crosby recorded it in 1962. (All footnotes were added by the editor.)

"*Shih,*" she said.

"Is he good to you or does he sometimes beat you?"

"Sometimes, when there are no men who want me. But he is good. If men do not want me, it is my fault. … Why do you not want me?"

"I am tired," I said. "I have traveled a long way and swiftly. I wished merely to sit for a moment and gaze upon beauty before continuing my journey. I paid your man below so that I might descend partway to heaven with you."

She giggled again, bobbing her head like a perplexed goose. "You don't talk like the men who come here," she said. "They only swear and grunt like pigs. Are there many men like you in the world?"

"Here and there," I said. "But they do not live long, unless they find a refuge such as this and one like you who understands their madness."

I was talking without paying attention to what I said, my ears straining to hear the sounds below and the fingers of one hand touching the gun beneath my arm. But the man below stuck to his story, and my pursuers sounded satisfied. Then I heard the steps going away.

I continued to talk to her in the flowery language for which Chinese is so perfect, but I also continued to listen. After a while I heard the motor of an approaching car, and then it stopped. A moment later the basket began to move downward.

I still couldn't be sure, so I kept my hand on the gun until we were low enough for me to recognize Jimmy Shan. Then the basket bumped to a stop on the ground. I opened the door and stepped out. I turned to the girl.

"Petal of the lotus blossom," I said, "you will never know to what heights you have carried me this night. I have returned to earth renewed and reborn, and I will forever remember that it was only with you that I truly saw the stars."

She giggled but raised her head quickly. *"Ni shih hao jen,"* she said, and then quickly ducked her head again in embarrassment.

I went to the car and got in. Jimmy Shan got in beside me. As I drove away, I got a glimpse of the pimp ordering the girl from the cage and pulling down his rope. Business had been good and he was going home. Business had been good for me and I was going home, too.

I was still laughing part of the way home, but I finally stopped. Then I thought of something.

"Jimmy," I said, "how did it happen that you were there tonight? Did you follow me again?"

"No," he said. "I was already there. I had a whisper from someone that tonight those men would kill a man at Kai Shing's. Knowing that they were men who interested you, I went to see what would happen. When you came in, I knew that it was you they meant to kill. The rest was easy. I know Kai Shing's. I have been there many times, and seen a man drugged and then carried out as though he were merely drunk and being taken home by kind friends. Always he would be found in the water the next day."

"This is twice you have saved my life," I said. "How do I repay you?"

"It is nothing," he said.

"We'll see," I answered.

When we reached the hotel, I paid Jimmy the money I owed him and went in. As I crossed the lobby, the night clerk looked up and called to me. I went over to the desk.

"Someone called you only a few minutes ago, Mr. March," he said. "He seemed most anxious to talk to you, and asked that we give you his name and number no matter what time you came in."

"Who was it?"

He reached up and pulled a telephone message slip from the row of boxes. He gave it to me. The name on it was Frank Burney.

"Thanks," I said. I went on upstairs to my room. I took off the gun and holster and put them away in the dresser. I made myself a good strong drink, then picked up the phone. I gave the operator Frank Burney's number. He answered on the second ring.

"Frank," I said, "this is Milo."

"Where are you?" he asked excitedly.

"I just got back to the hotel and found your message."

"God, I was worried about you. What happened?"

"Someone came by and tipped me off that those five men were there to get me," I said. "I went out the back way. Sorry to leave you like that, but I was told that they wouldn't bother you if I wasn't with you."

"You were gone when I went back to the table," he said. "The waiter told me you'd gone to the men's room. But then Blake and West and the three Chinese got up and left in a hurry. I went back to the men's room to look for you, but you weren't there. And I couldn't get any information about you, so finally I came home. And, you know, there was something else funny about it."

"What?"

"That beer I had. I only drank half a bottle, but I've been feeling very strange. Sleepy and half sick to my stomach."

"The drinks were drugged," I told him. "You probably didn't get enough to do any damage. The best thing for you is to go to bed and sleep it off. I'll call you tomorrow."

"Okay," he said. "It's a big relief to find out that you're all right. I was beginning to feel responsible."

"I'm hard to kill," I said. "Good night, Frank."

I hung up, finished my drink, and got into bed. Then I had an idea. I turned the light on again and looked at my watch. It was a little after three. I picked up the phone and made another call. The line was busy, so I put the phone down, said to hell with it, and turned out the light. I was asleep almost as soon as I closed my eyes.

I didn't awaken the next morning until ten o'clock. Even then, what brought me out of bed was somebody knocking on the door. I walked over to it.

"Who is it?" I asked.

"Jimmy."

I unlocked the door and headed for the bed, calling back over my shoulder, "Come on in." I was in bed by the time he came in with his usual cheerful smile.

"Don't you ever sleep?" I grumbled.

"Sure," he said. "I had plenty of sleep. You want to sleep more?"

"A lot of good it would do me if I did," I said. "No, I've got to get to work anyway. This is my fifth day in this crummy place, and all I've done is provide a target for someone. Sit down and relax."

I picked up the phone and called room service, ordering my usual breakfast plus some ice. I lit a cigarette and stared glumly at Jimmy Shan until the waiter arrived. After I signed for the meal, he left. I poured myself a drink and motioned to Jimmy. "Help yourself."

He did with alacrity.

"No little surprises for me this morning?" I asked. "No new millionaires robbed or anything like that?"

He shook his head. "News very dull this morning. Police still report they expect to make early arrest, but offer no new facts. No news in the paper about last night."

"If there were, we probably wouldn't be reading it," I said. "I'm getting too old for this kind of life. I think I'll settle down on a chicken farm."

"Chickens are very nice," he said politely.

"Yeah—especially when they're in Moo Goo Gai Pan. I don't suppose you've picked up any more information this morning?"

"No."

"Then what the hell are you doing here?" I asked. His smile grew broader.

"I detected the same tone in your voice last night. I think it means that action starts today, so I came around for orders."

"You're too damn smart," I told him. I finished my drink and tackled the breakfast. "The only trouble is I don't have any orders at the moment. Stick around."

When I reached coffee and a second cigarette, I began to feel a little more human. I picked up the phone and called Inspector Hemming.

"Good morning," I said when he came on. "This is Milo March. How goes everything with all the professional snoopers this morning?"

"Fine," he said evenly. "Does your call mean that you've finally got more than a guess?"

"No. Everything was quiet last night." I winked at Jimmy. "I was wondering if anything was happening on your end."

"We're working," he said. "I expect we'll have something before long. Was that all, Mr. March?"

"That's all," I said cheerfully. "Just wanted to make sure you were keeping on your toes. Cheerio."

I depressed the bar for a second, then released it, and told the operator that I wanted to call Po Hing but I didn't have his number. She got the number and put the call through. I spoke to a couple of characters before I finally got him.

"Hiya, pal," he said. "I thought maybe I'd hear from you yesterday, after you got through with the cop."

"I was busy."

He chuckled. "So I heard."

"What do you mean?"

"My boys get around," he said. "And after what happened here night before last, I decided maybe I was interested in that Whitey Blake. I put some of my boys on it. They called once last night to tell me that Blake had some plans about you. At Kai Shing's."

"Seems to me they were able to get a lot of information there."

"They ought to be able to. I own the joint."

"You own it?" I exclaimed. "Then that waiter that put mickeys in our drinks is one of your boys, too?"

"Well, not exactly. He works in the joint, that's all. You know how it is. I don't mind any of them doing a little work on the side, as long as it doesn't interfere with me. I had a little talk with that waiter this morning. You can go back anytime you want to and all you'll get is straight drinks."

"No thanks."

"Anyway," he continued, "when the boys called, I told them to stick around and if you needed any help to give you a hand. But they told me you handled it real smart."

"Thanks," I said. "Everybody's trying to save my life. I'm overcome."

"It's all on the house," he said. "You did me a favor yesterday. What did you do with the souvenir?"

"I've still got it," I said. "I was thinking of giving it back to its rightful owner, if you have no objections."

"None. I had it longer than I wanted it. As I told you, I'm sticking to my own racket. But maybe that Whitey Blake won't be bothering you anymore in a couple of days."

"No," I said sharply. "He's mine."

"What?"

"I said he's mine. I've got first claim on him, and I don't want you or anyone else trying to cut in ahead of me."

"Okay," he said. "But if you have any trouble, give me a call."

"I don't think it'll be necessary," I said. "One way or another, I expect to clear it up today and get out of here tomorrow."

"You're that close?" he asked.

"Yes."

"Okay, pal. Good luck. And that's the first time I ever said that to any kind of a cop."

"Thanks, Hing. I'll call you before I leave." I hung up and thought for a minute. Finally, I turned to Jimmy.

"That first night when you came here," I said, "you knew all about my visit to the police and to Burney's office and what was said in both places. How did you find out?"

He smiled. "The receptionist in Burney's office. She likes to go out on the town once in a while and I take her. Then there's a clerk who works in the police station who doesn't make enough money. He's discovered that listening at doors sometimes increases his income."

"You have other arrangements like that?"

"Sure."

"Is there a lot of that going on in Hong Kong?"

"Sure. Every person I pay off is probably taking money from five or six others. It's one of the biggest businesses in Hong Kong."

"Well," I said, "I don't want anyone to think I'm bluffing." I picked up the phone and called the desk. I asked them to get me a reservation on Pan American to New York for the next day. After that I called Burney. He was in.

"How are you feeling today?" I asked when he came on.

"As if I had a hangover," he said. "Otherwise all right. Anything up?"

"Not much. Had any more reports on Blake and West?"

"I have the reports from yesterday during the day and the

early part of the night, but there's nothing in them. I have a report on the latter part of the night, but you and I were there."

"I guess we were," I said. "Well, I think you might as well call your men off."

"What?"

"Call them off. The agency is still on the payroll, but today will be the last day."

"I don't understand," he said. "Are you giving up?"

"No," I said cheerfully. "I expect to wind the case up today and leave Hong Kong tomorrow."

"How? What's happened?"

"Nothing yet—but it will. I'll be in to see you before I leave." I broke the connection.

My next call was to Hsu Chin Kwang. The houseboy seemed doubtful that the old man would speak to me and explained that the daughter was not there, but Hsu soon answered.

"March *hsien*," he said. "It is most thoughtful of you to telephone. I trust you are well."

"Very well," I said. "And you?"

"How well can an old man be?" he replied. "But I will go to my ancestors when it is destined."

"So it is written," I agreed gravely. "Is there any word about your jade?"

"No. I am told by the police that they expect to have word any hour, but I have heard nothing."

"Through circumstances which I cannot relate," I said, "one of the pieces taken from your house has come into my hands. It will be an honor to return it to you."

"You do me too much honor," he said, and I could hear the note of caution in his voice. "Perhaps there have been expenses involved in recovering it. If such is the case, I will be glad to pay—"

"No, no," I interrupted. "There were no expenses, and I consider myself the most favored of people in being able to return it. I myself will shortly tell the police that I have returned this piece."

"I understand," he said.

"I have reason to believe that the other pieces will be returned very soon," I said. "I trust they will then remain with you to brighten the rest of your days."

"You have information?" he asked.

"Yes. The theft of your jade is related to the theft of the other jade for which I have been looking. I expect to recover all of it in less than twenty-four hours."

We spent another two minutes flattering each other and each other's ancestors before I was finally able to hang up.

"That was some performance," Jimmy Shan said when I finished. "I'll bet he ate it up. Those old boys always do. I've heard some of them go on about who was the most honored for half a day."

"I rather enjoy it myself," I said, "when I'm not in a hurry. Well, I've got a couple more calls to make." I picked up the phone again and called Mei Hsu's apartment. She was there.

"Milo," she said, "I'm so glad to hear from you. How was it last night?"

"Very dull," I said. "I've been in worse dives in New York. How is my Mandarin princess today?"

"Lonely and waiting for you to call. Are you coming over?"

"Not now, honey. It's going to be a very busy day. But I'll see you sometime. I have to, because I'm going back to New York tomorrow."

There was a moment of silence. "Just when I've found you? That's not fair. Why are you leaving so soon?"

"Oh, I expect to wind the case up today and get back all the missing jade. When the job's over, I have to go back."

"The first part is wonderful, but the last is horrible. What has happened? You must tell me all about it."

"Later."

"But I will see you?"

"You'll see me," I said. "Good-bye, honey." I depressed the bar on the phone.

Then I called Burney's office again and asked for Linda McKay.

"Milo March," I said, when she came on. "How are you?"

"Busy," she said. "Some new work came into the office. But I'm never too busy to talk to my favorite man. How did it go last night?"

"Routine stuff. Nothing very startling."

"I know better," she said. "Frank told me about the drugged drinks and that those men had planned to kill you. How did you ever manage to lose them?"

"It was easy," I said. "I just flew up into the air until they went away."

"I don't understand …"

"I'll explain it later."

"Am I going to see you tonight?"

"You'll see me," I said. "In fact, this will be the last night I can see you. I'm going back to New York tomorrow."

"But I thought you said nothing happened last night."

"It didn't. It's all going to happen today. And as soon as I get back the jade and turn the gang over to the cops, the job will be over. But I'll see you later."

"I'll wait," she said.

I replaced the phone and poured myself a fresh drink. I motioned to Jimmy to help himself. He did. He returned to his chair and looked at me.

"You told them all the same thing," he said.

"Yes."

"You think that one of them is the person you're looking for?"

"I'm pretty certain of it. But even if I'm wrong, maybe one of them will talk and it will reach the right person."

"And then?"

"Another attempt will be made to get rid of me. Only this time it won't be a surprise. I'll be waiting for it. Enjoy your drink. I'm going to take a shower."

I went into the bathroom and showered and shaved. I got dressed, then took my gun from the dresser. I removed the clip and ejected the one bullet in the chamber. I took a rag and carefully cleaned the gun. I put the clip back in and pumped a shell into the chamber and flipped on the safety.

I had some adhesive tape in my suitcase. I got it out, rolled up my pants leg, and taped the gun to my leg just beneath the knee in the back. I rolled down the pants leg.

Jimmy had been watching all of this silently. "You know,"

he said dreamily, "I could probably sell all of this for a very high price. All I would have to do is get in touch with Whitey Blake."

"Sure," I said. "I thought about that. But there are two things about it."

"What?"

"First, you've sat here watching me set a trap for someone. But you have no way of knowing that I'm not also setting a trap for you. I might have some other plan altogether."

"And the second thing?"

"I don't believe in very many people," I said, "but I believe you wouldn't do it. I don't think you could save my life twice and then sell me out even if the price were right."

He smiled broadly. "That is true, but how can you be sure?"

"I can't, but there is another thing. You don't know yet whether I will reward you afterwards or not—or how much the reward will be if I give one to you. It might be more than the others would pay; it might be less. But I think you're a gambler."

"So are you," he said. "It's your life."

"Yeah, I read the small print, too," I said. "You've been waiting for orders. Now I'm ready to give them to you. I don't want you around here. It might even spoil the trap. On the other hand, there is the possibility that my guess is wrong, and I don't want to have to set the trap twice. So you go out and get busy. Spread the same story I told on the phone in places where it may get passed on. You can do that, can't you?"

"Yes," he said. "I can drop remarks where there will be

informers, but are you sure that you want me to? Wouldn't it be better if I stayed here with you?"

I shook my head. "It would tip off anybody that there was a trap. And, as I said, I might be off course. No, run along Jimmy. I'll see you later."

He stood up and stared at me with bright, inquisitive eyes. "You know," he said, "I think you will. I wasn't always sure before, but now I am. I'll see what I can do." He turned and left the room without looking back.

When he was gone, I sat down and poured myself a fresh drink. I knew it would probably be a long wait. I phoned down and asked them to send me up all the papers, a couple of magazines, and some ice. Then I relaxed.

The boy arrived with the papers, magazines, and the ice, also an airmail letter. I paid him and let him go, then opened the letter. It was the list from Robert Carlin of all the missing jade. I folded it and put it in my pocket.

I ran over what little planning I had done, and decided it was about as good as I could do on an ad-lib basis. Only a couple of little things were gnawing at my mind, but I was sure they would fall into place. There were things I could do to make sure about them, but I might miss the other show-down, and I wanted to get everything tied up neatly.

Finally, I put the whole thing out of my mind and started reading the papers. There wasn't anything very interesting. The world was still in the same mess it had been for some years. Everybody was doing a lot of talking about it, but that was about all. President Kennedy was meeting somebody in Europe for another summit meeting, and one by one the little countries were still being sold down the river. Locally, everyone was still wondering what Red China would do when Great Britain's lease on Hong Kong expired.* There were a few short stories on various local crimes. The society pages were more exciting and not nearly so stupid.

Noon came and I ordered some lunch sent up. I looked at the V.O. and told them to bring a double martini with it.

Finally, I had a bright idea while I was waiting for the food, and put in a phone call to Pan American. The waiter arrived while I was in the middle of it. I signed the check, added his tip, and went on with the call. When I'd finished, I drank the martini slowly, enjoying every sip of it. Then I tackled the food. It was equally good.

It's a funny thing. For the past four days, when nothing was happening, I was as jumpy as hell; but now that I thought something was going to take place, I felt fine. Part of the reason was that this was the way I work best. All this business about deduction is a lot of nonsense. There are only two ways to solve a case. One is by plugging hard work, and that's not for me. The other is to start pushing and wait to see who pushes back. That's my system, and it's always worked pretty well.

After I finished lunch, I switched from papers to magazines. They were pretty dull, but I read along as if they were the most exciting thing I'd ever seen. I had a couple more drinks. The whiskey tasted fine, but it wasn't making me the least bit drunk. That's when drinking is fun.

---

* The People's Republic of China resumed sovereignty over Hong Kong in 1997 after more than a century of British rule.

At about two o'clock the phone rang. I picked it up and said hello.

"Hiya, pal," the voice said. I recognized the expression, if not the voice. It was Po Hing.

"Hello, Hing," I said.

"What's cooking?" he asked.

"The same stew."

"And you're just sitting there?" he asked. "I'm not even in it, and I'm getting jumpy just sitting here and listening to the radio. What are you doing?"

"Waiting for someone to make a move."

"Want me to send a couple of boys over to the hotel? Just to hang around like, in case they're needed?"

"No," I said firmly. "Thanks, Hing, but it might spoil everything. I know what I'm doing, and I can handle it."

"Okay, pal," he said. "I was only trying to help."

"I know," I said. "Thanks, Hing."

"Yeah," he said. "I'll see you around." He broke the connection.

I went back to thinking, going over everything I knew, guessed, or thought might happen. I knew that any way it went, it would be close—but I liked it.

Having reassured myself, I went back to the magazines. There was a fascinating piece on the botanical gardens of Hong Kong. The phone rang again. I was almost glad that it interrupted my reading. I picked it up and said hello.

"Milo," he said, "this is Frank Burney. I wasn't sure you'd be there, but I thought I'd try."

"I'm here," I said.

"How are things going?"

"Fine."

"Is Linda with you?"

He surprised me with that. "No. Why?"

"She never came back from lunch. She was supposed to finish some work here. I—I thought she might have been in touch with you."

"I spoke to her earlier," I said, "and I'm supposed to call her later, but that's all I know. She'll probably show up."

"I don't know," he said worriedly. "I'm a little concerned. She's usually very responsible."

"If I hear from her, I'll let you know," I said, "or I'll tell her to get in touch with you."

"Thanks, Milo. Are you going to be there?"

"For a while."

"Okay, then, I'll talk to you." He hung up.

I went back to the botanical gardens and waiting.

It was maybe a half hour later that the knock came on the door. I put the magazine to one side and poured myself a drink. The knock was repeated.

"Come in," I called.

The door opened and Eddie West stepped inside. Whitey Blake came in after him and closed the door. Both of them were smiling as if they had a private joke.

"Hello, sucker," Eddie West said.

"I don't think I know you," I said. "I do know the hood with you, but not you."

"I'm Eddie West. You'll get to know me better before the day is over won't he, Whitey?"

"Yeah," Whitey said. He was staring at me with those blue-white eyes. "I owe you something, March."

"Not a thing, Whitey," I said. "I'd do the same thing for you again, or for any of your friends. It was my pleasure."

"It's going to be our pleasure now," he said.

"What is?"

"We're going to take a little trip, just the three of us," Eddie West said. "A nice little walk down through the lobby, then a nice car ride through the city."

"You make it sound enchanting," I said. "What makes you think that I want to go with you? Or will? I know about you two cheap punks. I think I could probably take both of you any day in the week."

"Yeah?" Eddie West said. He grinned at me. "We don't have to use any strong-arm stuff. You're a busy little bee, March. You only been here for five days, and already you've got two broads on the string. You like broads, don't you, March?"

"They're pretty nice, but you probably wouldn't know. What about the two broads?"

"We've got them," he said. "Both of them. We're going to take you to see them, but if you don't want to come, then we'll go away, and then every day we'll send you a piece of one of the broads. How do you like that, March?"

EIGHT

So that was going to be their move. I'd known that they would probably come for me, but I'd thought it would be strictly strong-arm stuff. This was their solution for getting me out of the hotel and through the streets, without anything to show what was going on. It had a certain kind of cleverness. I almost liked it.

"I don't think too much of it," I said evenly. "But why pick on the two girls? They haven't done anything to you."

"No, but we'll do something to them, if you don't come along without a fuss. We've got three Chink partners—you saw them the other night in Kai Shing's. You know how Chinks are about things like that."

"Tell me something," I said gravely. "I've always been curious about it. Is it true that when a Chinese cuts someone's throat, he cuts it up and down instead of across?"

"The guy's a card," Eddie West said. "Maybe we ought to shuffle him up a little."

"He's also tricky," Whitey Blake said. "We shouldn't take no chances with him."

"Okay," Eddie said. He pulled out a gun. "Stand up, sucker."

I stood up.

"Take a look, Whitey," Eddie said.

Whitey Blake came over to me, being careful not to get between me and the gun. He ran his hands over my chest and waist and patted my pockets.

"He's not carrying anything," he said. He went back to stand beside his partner.

Eddie put his gun away. "How come, March?" he asked. "You're one of them private dicks, and I thought they always carried guns."

"You've been watching too much television, Eddie," I said. "I carry a gun sometimes, when it's in a place where I have a permit. I don't have one here, and that makes a gun illegal. So—no gun."

"That's what I like about cops: They're so law-abiding. Think how tough it would be if they was like us. Well, what about it, March?"

"What about what?"

"You coming with us nice and peaceable—or do we start sending you a few choice pieces of the two broads?"

"You coming, March?" Whitey asked.

"I'll come," I said. "Of course, if I come, you'll let the two girls go?"

"Well, not right away. We'll have to keep them until we've finished our little talk with you. But nothing will happen to them. We give you our word on that." Eddie grinned at me, as if to say that the three of us knew how good their word was. But then he thought he had me over a barrel, and so it didn't make any difference.

"Okay," I said. "I guess I don't have much choice. Do you mind if I put on my coat?"

"Check it, Whitey."

Whitey moved across the room and went through my coat, which was hanging on the back of a chair. He nodded when he'd finished. I went over and put it on. Whitey opened the door.

"Let's go, sucker," Eddie said. "You first, but we'll be right with you. Don't try anything that the broads will be sorry for."

The phone began to ring.

"Forget it, sucker," Eddie said. "There ain't anybody home. Just get moving."

I went through the door and they followed me. We rode down in the elevator and walked through the lobby like three old buddies out for a stroll. They had a car parked a half block from the hotel. Eddie and I got in the back, while Whitey drove.

We went through the main part of Hong Kong, headed toward North Point, but just after we passed Happy Valley we turned off. Then, not long after we passed Ching Man Village, the car pulled up in front of an old house. The three of us got out and went inside.

There was quite a collection there in the living room. Mei Hsu and Linda McKay were both there, each one tied to a chair. Then there were five Chinese, three of them the men I had seen the night before. The other two were more roughly dressed and tougher-looking. One of them was using a knife with a six-inch blade to pick his teeth.

"Milo," Mei said as I came in, "I'm sorry. I didn't know they were going to use me for this. I thought they merely wanted ransom from my father."

"It's all right, honey," I told her. "Have they mistreated either one of you?"

"No."

"Milo," Linda said then, and it sounded as though she was on the verge of tears, "what is this? Are these the men … you were looking for?"

"Yes," I said.

"And he found us," Eddie West said, laughing. "He's a very smart dick, that March."

"What are we going to do, Milo?" Linda asked.

"Have a chat," I said. "I believe that's what the boys told me they wanted."

"Sure, that's what we want," Eddie said. "Sit down, March, and we'll see how good you talk."

I looked around the room. There were plenty of chairs, and I finally picked one that had its back to the wall facing the rest of the room. It was a big, comfortable-looking chair, and I hoped they'd think that was the reason I'd picked it "Not as young as I used to be," I said as I sat down, "and these comfortable chairs look mighty inviting."

"On the other hand," Eddie said, "you're about as old as you'll ever be. … Turn that radio off."

One of the Chinese went over and turned off the radio, which had been playing softly. As he did so, I heard someone moving around in the next room.

"If we're going to talk," I said, "don't you think that everyone should be in on it?"

"What do you mean?"

I nodded toward the other room. "I just think that Frank

could hear better if he came in here."

Eddie West laughed. The door to the other room opened and Frank Burney came in, scowling.

"I suppose you think you're pretty smart," he said.

"Reasonably so," I said, "all things considered. But I didn't have to be too smart to know that you were in this, and that it was probably you who was in the next room."

"Frank!" Linda McKay said. "Frank! I—I thought you were a prisoner, too, when you came through that door. … You're one of them!"

"Yes, dear partner," he said. "Does it surprise you?" He turned back to me. "When did you get the idea that I was in this?"

"At Kai Shing's—although I was beginning to suspect something before. West and Blake were being too pure, according to your reports. But then you set that thing up at Kai Shing's. Sorry, Frank, it was just too obvious when I started to think about it."

"How?" he persisted.

"Do I wound your ego?" I asked. "Well, it's true that a couple of other people knew I was going to Kai Shing's, but then you also swore that Blake and West didn't contact anyone else all day. Yet they came there specifically to get me. You were going to be drugged, too, so that there wouldn't be any suspicion of you. There was probably less of the drug in your beer, but even so, you left the table on the pretext of talking to your agent so that I'd have a chance to get ahead of you in drinking. If you'd been on the up-and-up, that would have been a stupid thing to do. Since you were with me, they would have noticed. As it was, they paid no attention at all. Then, when I seemed to get out of the trap, you hurried back home and put in a call to me at the hotel. If I succeeded in getting away, you wanted to find out what I had learned and to alibi yourself as much as you could."

"Frank," Linda said again, "I can't believe it."

"Oh, shut up," he said. He looked at me again. "That was clever of you, March. But it was certainly a piece of luck for us when you came in to hire me."

"It was lucky for me, too," I said. "Otherwise I might not have known that it was you who masterminded the attempt on me last night. It was also you who hired Chan Chok How to try to kill me the first night I was here, wasn't it?"

"Yes. You were the first one to think that we were operating out of Hong Kong, and we had to get rid of you."

"And when Chan Chok How failed, you had him killed. If I'd really been on my toes, I would have guessed it was you. Oh, I suppose when Whitey Blake failed to get me in New York, he sent back word and you were alerted. But I arrived here and talked to only three people. Inspector Simmons, you, and one other person. And immediately there was a second attempt to get me. You were the only one it could have been. And it was also you who had Whitey hire Thomas Luk to try to kill me the other night."

There was a grunt of surprise from one of the Chinese. "That's Thomas Luk," Frank Burney said. "How'd you know his name? I don't suppose it really matters now."

"Not much," I said. "Everything you did fit into the pattern, once I started thinking about you. Even your call this afternoon, pretending you were worried about Linda. That was setting it up so I'd believe it, when the two hoods waltzed in and said they had her. You were very efficient—and about as clever as a Cub Scout on his first patrol."

He scowled again. "It's funny that I was so stupid and you so clever, but I've got you and not the other way around. I suppose it was you that managed somehow to upset the frame on Po Hing?"

"Yes. I have the piece of jade you stashed there, and it will be returned to Miss Hsu's father. And that wasn't very smart, Burney. Even if you don't get locked up right away, Po Hing has a long memory."

"Who cares?" he said. "Po Hing is small-time."

"Maybe," I said. "You know, there's only one thing that bothers me. This whole jade operation was a smart one, and you seem to be so stupid. How do you explain that?"

Eddie West laughed again, and Burney's face darkened. "I'll show you who's stupid before I'm through with you."

"Everybody talks too damn much," one of the Chinese said. It was the one Jimmy had told me was called Ma Tsing.

"You're right, Ma," Whitey Blake said. "Especially with this guy March. If you let him talk, you can be damn sure he's planning something while he's doing it."

"You ought to know," Burney said. "If you hadn't bungled the job in New York, there wouldn't have been any trouble here."

"You have to expect a few bungles," I said. "However, it did work pretty well up to now. What did you do—case each job, then plan it here and send either two or three people to carry it out? An expert at breaking and entering, a gun, and a carrier. Sometimes, as in the last Rome job, the gun and the carrier doubled."

"So it was you who put the slug on me in my apartment," Eddie West said. "Now I owe you something, too."

"Now, why," I asked Burney, "did you pull the robbery of Hsu Chin Kwang? It was the first time you'd fouled your own nest. Was it just to get stuff to hang a frame on Po Hing? Or was somebody smart enough to know that I suspected Hsu Chin Kwang, and hoped that this would make me believe that he was trying to be smart?"

"What the hell is this?" Whitey Blake asked irritably. "We bring the guy here to ask him some questions before we knock him off, and all that happens is that he keeps asking the questions."

I looked at them while Whitey was talking. There were eight of them, which made the odds a little steeper than I had bargained on. But I knew that it couldn't be too long before I would have to make my play. And I'd have only one chance.

"Look at him," Eddie West said. "You got to give him one thing. He's got guts. He's sitting there, looking at us and wondering if he can take us. It's eight to one on the surface. But that ain't all. We all got guns or knives. That makes it at least sixteen to one. You ever think of that, March?"

I shrugged. "I've played longer odds at the track."

"Yeah, but this ain't no two-dollar window," he said. "Let's get it over with. Find out what we have to, and Whitey and I will flip a coin to see who takes him."

"I think you're right," Burney said. He turned to me. "Have

you filed any reports while you've been here, March?"

"Why should I tell you anything?" I asked. "You're making it quite clear that you intend to kill me, so what do I buy?"

"I thought the boys told you," Burney said. "If you want to clam up on us, you can sit there and watch us carve up the two girls until it loosens your tongue."

"Don't tell them anything," Mei said. "They won't dare do anything to us, Milo."

"Tom," Burney said.

Thomas Luk moved quickly across the room and his knife flashed once. The blade slipped neatly under one shoulder of Linda's blouse, cutting it and her brassiere strap. The blouse and the brassiere flopped down, baring one shoulder and a beautifully formed breast.

"Milo," Linda cried.

"A man that clever with a knife," Frank Burney said, "can do a lot of cutting without actually killing a person."

"Mr. March," said Ma Tsing, "seems familiar with the language and customs of my country. Perhaps he has heard of the Death of a Thousand Cuts, which was once popular among my people. Thomas Luk is an expert at it."

"They wouldn't dare, Milo," Mei Hsu said again. "They know my father. If they do anything to me, he will make sure that they die in a way that will make the Death of a Thousand Cuts seem pleasant."

"Your father is an old man," Ma Tsing said insolently, "and he has traded his courage for playthings."

"Tom," Burney said again.

Thomas Luk grinned and stepped in again. This time he

slashed at Mei's dress and the top half of it fell, leaving her nude to the waist. She shrank back against the chair.

"You got to say one thing for this March guy," Eddie West said. "He's got good taste in broads."

Everybody's attention was momentarily on Mei Hsu. I took advantage of it to loosen the adhesive that was holding the gun to my leg. And I pulled my pants leg a little higher, so that the cuff was just below the gun.

"Enough of this," Ma Tsing suddenly said. "Get on with it."

This took me by surprise. He'd said no more than a few sentences before this, and I had been thinking that Frank Burney was in charge. But now Ma Tsing was clearly giving an order.

"Okay," Burney said. "You want to answer the question, March, or you want to see more of Tom Luk's ability?"

I looked them over again. I knew the time was drawing near when I'd have to make a move, but if I guessed the wrong time, it could be fatal.

"Don't try it, March," Eddie West said. "Even if you were a good enough man to get us, there are four more outside."

"Let him try it," Ma Tsing said. "You searched him, didn't you?"

"Yeah."

"Then let him try. It might be amusing."

"Okay," I said wearily. "I haven't sent any reports, except they know that I think the ring is operating from here."

"You called me," Burney said, "and told me that you expected to clear the case up today. What made you so sure?"

"I was bluffing."

"You're lying," Burney said. "We know that you're lying."

"You made a reservation on the plane for tomorrow," Ma Tsing said. He sounded as if he was getting impatient. "Why?"

"I thought my bluff would work."

"Tom," Burney said again.

Thomas Luk made another pass with his knife, and the second half of Linda's blouse fell away. Now there were two pairs of bare breasts, one pair like ivory and the other like peaches and cream. I took advantage of the distraction to tear loose the adhesive, bending my leg back so that the gun was held in the vise of my knee.

"The next time," Burney said, "it won't be cloth."

"Don't tell them," Mei said again. "It will make no difference. They will kill us, too, once they have killed you. I'm not afraid."

"I am afraid," Linda said, without taking her eyes off the knife, "but don't tell them, Milo."

"It's all right," I said. "I don't mind telling them. It was partly bluff. But I did know that you were in it, Burney. And I knew that Blake and West and Ma Tsing were in it, but I didn't know if that was all or not. And I didn't really have any proof. So I decided to push a little and see what happened. That's all."

"What did you tell the police?"

"Nothing."

"Did you tell anyone else who you suspected?"

"No."

"You're the only one who knows this?"

"Yes."

"Well, I think that's it," Burney said.

"Let's get it over with," Eddie West said. "We can fix it so it'll look real neat to the cops. He's been chasing around with both broads. So one of them catches him with the other, and there's a general fight in which they all get killed."

"Wait," Ma Tsing said. "You have the jade from Po Hing's house. Where is it now?"

"In my hotel room."

"That could work out very well," Burney said. "We can make it look as if March robbed the old man night before last. There have been crooked insurance dicks before."

"Just like crooked private detectives," I said.

"There is one other thing which interests me," Ma Tsing said. "At first you refused to answer any questions. Perhaps you like the two girls, but I was watching your face, and I do not think you were frightened when we said we would cut them. But you still started talking freely. Why?"

There was the sound of a car motor somewhere outside, and it suddenly gave me an idea.

"I was waiting for the police," I said.

"The police?" Burney asked. He turned and ran to a window.

Then I got a break I wasn't expecting. There was the sound of a gunshot outside, followed by a whole fusillade. I straightened my leg and let the gun fall, grabbing it with one hand and throwing myself to the floor.

The shots had taken everyone's attention except Eddie West's. He'd been expecting me to make a break for it ever since we'd gotten there, and he was still watching. He went for his gun as I made my move. It had barely cleared the holster when I hit the floor. I shot him through the right shoulder and his gun dropped.

I shifted my attention to Whitey Blake. He'd heard the shot in the room and was turning fast, but I still had plenty of time. I took good aim and shot him through one knee. He screamed with pain and went down, the gun skidding away from him.

After that, things became a blur. There was more shooting outside and I heard someone shouting. Inside, it was worse. A lot of attention was suddenly focused on me. Frank Burney snapped a shot at me that almost got me. I did get him. I wasn't sure where, but I was trying to keep them all alive and so I had aimed for his shoulder. All I knew was that he dropped. There was no time to check on the results. I shot one of the Chinese somewhere in the chest. Then something hit me in the left shoulder and stung like hell. I could feel a trickle of warmth down my chest.

I shot another Chinese, desperately aware even as I pulled the trigger that Ma Tsing was across the room with his gun lined up on me. I rolled on the floor and brought my gun up, knowing I'd be too late. But I wasn't. When my gaze finally found Ma Tsing, he was falling to the floor. The handle of a knife stuck out from his throat, the blood spurting around it.

I looked around the room. There were still two Chinese on their feet. One was already running for the door. The other was grappling with Jimmy Shan, and even as I looked, Jimmy slipped a knife between his ribs.

I sent a shot after the running Chinese and he stopped, throwing his hands over his head.

"Where'd you come from, Jimmy?" I asked.

He gave me that broad smile. "I thought you might like to see me about now," he said, "so I came through the window."

"Thanks," I said. I nodded toward where Ma Tsing lay. "This is the third time you've saved my life."

Before he could answer, the door suddenly flew open and the place was full of police. Leading them was Inspector Hemming. He scowled around the room.

"I was never so glad to see a cop in my life," I said. "Welcome to the party."

"Looks more like a slaughterhouse," he said. "Couldn't you have waited a few more minutes until I got here?"

"Didn't know you were coming," I said. "And things got a little out of hand."

I was suddenly aware that my shoulder was hurting like hell. I looked down at it and was surprised to see the handle of a knife protruding from my coat. I just stared at it, not being sure what I should do.

"That should come out," Jimmy Shan said, coming over and kneeling in front of me. He put one hand on the knife handle and the other on my shoulder. "Steady, now." He pulled, and for a minute the pain was worse. Then the knife was in his hand, the blade red with my blood.

Jimmy pulled a handkerchief from his breast pocket. "We'd better try to stop the blood until you can get to a doctor," he said. "I'll try to fasten this to your shoulder some way."

I glanced down at the gun which was still in my right hand, and laughed. "I brought my own adhesive tape," I said, and handed the gun, with the tape still on it, to him.

As he went to work on my shoulder, I could see two police-men freeing the girls and wrapping their coats around them. Others were getting the prisoners to their feet. All except two. Jimmy Shan hadn't been fooling with his two. They were both dead. One of them was Ma Tsing.

Inspector Hemming had stopped to look at the two dead men, then walked over to me. "Well," he said, "we've got six live ones. Who's this fellow?"

"Jimmy Shan," I said. "He's been helping me. As a matter of fact, today is the third time he's saved my life. I didn't know he was going to be here today, but I guess he followed me. It's a habit he seems to have. Is that what you did, Jimmy?"

"Yes," he said. "I did what you told me to, and then went back and waited outside the hotel. When you came out, I followed."

"Why didn't you call the police?" Inspector Hemming demanded.

"I did," Jimmy said, "as soon as I knew where they took Milo."

"Then it was you," Hemming said. He looked at me. "We got an anonymous tip on the phone. That's why we're here. I suppose this Jimmy Shan is responsible for the knife work?"

"His knife, my gun," I said.

"A bloody mess," the Inspector said. "Both of those chaps are dead. Serious matter."

"Oh, come on, now, Inspector," I said. "They were both criminals, part of the ring I told you about. Jimmy only killed them to keep them from killing us. It's self-defense, and you know it."

"I expect," Hemming said. "I wasn't talking about charging him. But look what a mess happens when you amateurs—excuse me—you unofficial chaps try to do something. You should have called me. What about your promise of cooperation?"

"I didn't have anything to tell you," I said. "I tried a bluff, and I didn't know who was going to call it. When I did know, I was hardly in a position to go to the phone."

"Of course," Hemming said coldly. "Who was your other confederate?"

"What other confederate?" I asked in surprise. "I don't have any. I came here alone. Jimmy followed me because he's gotten in the habit of protecting me. But that's all."

"Well, when we came up, some men were charging this house and shooting. They killed four men. Then they saw us coming and got away in a sedan. But we have the license number."

"I don't know anything about them," I said. Actually, I had an idea, but I wasn't going to tell Hemming.

"We'll see," he said. "I notice Frank Burney was among the wounded. Was he protecting you, too?"

"No. He's part of the gang."

"I see that white-haired chap is among them, and his friend West. Both with records. I know some of those China boys, too." He looked around the room again, shaking his head. "A bloody mess. Well, what's the story?"

I quickly told him the things I knew and what had gone on in the room. The two girls corroborated the latter part.

"And where's all this jewelry you keep talking about?" he asked.

"I don't know," I admitted. "We still have to find it. Maybe one of the men will talk."

"Well," he said, "we'll have to have statements from all of you down at headquarters."

"Inspector," I said, "I'm wounded and should get some medical attention. The two girls have been through a pretty shocking experience, and they are hardly properly clothed to go to the station. Surely we can come down later and give our statements."

"I suppose," he said glumly. He looked at Jimmy Shan. "You have any reason why you can't give a statement now?"

"No," Jimmy said cheerfully. "I'll be glad to, Inspector."

"Good," he said. "Shall we go?"

"Inspector," I said.

He looked at me.

"As I said, the girls have been through a very traumatic experience. Don't you think you and I should take them home?"

He looked at me for a minute, then nodded. "Quite," he said.

And that's the way it was done. Jimmy Shan went along with the other policemen and the prisoners. Inspector Hemming and the two girls and I got into another car and drove first to Mei Hsu's address.

"Inspector," I said, when we got there, "why don't you take Miss McKay home while I escort Miss Hsu up to her apartment? Then you can come back here and pick me up."

"Quite," he said again.

"I'll call you later, Linda," I said.

She merely nodded. She seemed still to be suffering from shock. The car drove off and Mei and I went upstairs.

"Let me look at your shoulder," she said as soon as we were in the apartment.

"No," I said. "It'll be all right until I get to a doctor."

"Milo," she said, putting her arms around my neck, but being careful of my shoulder, "you were wonderful. I was so frightened."

"You didn't show it, honey."

"I wouldn't give them the satisfaction," she said proudly. "Have you really been chasing around with that other girl?"

"I took her to dinner, that's all," I said. I was looking over her shoulder at the apartment, wondering where to start.

"I can be very jealous," she said. She kissed me on the cheek. "Do you believe in hunches?"

"Yes," I said, wondering if she knew how much I believed in hunches. "Why?"

"When did I meet you? Four days ago? Well, if I hadn't had a hunch, I would never have met you. I wouldn't have come back in time."

"Were you away?" I asked politely.

"I had been for several weeks. I only returned to Hong Kong two days before you arrived."

"Oh? Where were you?"

"Paris. I had been there seven weeks and had planned on staying another two weeks. Then I had a sudden hunch to come home and did so. And then two days later you showed up. Isn't it wonderful?"

"Did you say Paris?" I asked.

"Yes."

"And you were there for seven weeks?"

"Yes. But what's so unusual about that? I go to Paris every year."

"Can you prove that you were there for seven weeks and only came back two days before I arrived?"

"Of course I can, but why should I?"

I leaned down and kissed her. "Because I was about to make a blithering ass of myself. Honey, do you like jade?"

"I detest it," she said. "That's another thing that saddens my father. But I can't help it. I prefer diamonds and pearls— in case that's what you want to know. … But why all these strange questions?"

"I'll tell you later, honey," I said. I kissed her again, took the policeman's coat she'd been wearing, and went downstairs.

Inspector Hemming came along in a few minutes and picked me up.

"Inspector," I said as we drove away, "I have been an unmitigated idiot."

"Quite," he said amiably.

NINE

We drove along for several blocks in silence. I was thinking furiously and being annoyed with myself. After assuming first that Hsu Chin Kwang was the head of the ring, I'd had my grand hunch that his daughter was. Then it had seemed that everything fit—but mostly because I thought that it should. She was a tall, beautiful Chinese girl, so she was Mary Moy. The person who was the head of the ring needed money, and she had money. Her father knew about jade and had a collection, so therefore she must want one, too. And her father had wanted a boy, so she was trying to prove that she was a better bandit than he'd been. And so on and so on.

"Where shall I take you to see a doctor?" Inspector Hemming asked.

"No place," I snapped. "I'll see a doctor later. I want to go back to headquarters with you."

"Mind telling me what it's all about?" he asked mildly. "Or is this another guess?"

"We don't have all of the gang and we don't have the jade," I said. "I thought I knew the answer to both. I thought Mei Hsu was the head of the ring and the jade would be in that apartment of hers. That's why I had you take Linda McKay home while I went upstairs with Mei. I was going to come downstairs and hand the rest of the case to you. Then I found out that she was in Paris when I thought she was in America as Mary Moy."

"I could have told you that," he said. "You never asked."

"There were probably a lot of people who could have told me that," I said savagely, "but I never asked them. Including Mei herself. I had a neat little picture of the whole operation. Nine-tenths of it was right, but that's no excuse for accepting the other tenth on faith."

"True," he said. He sounded a little smug, but not too much so. Besides, I couldn't object, because I deserved it.

"Inspector," I said, "I want to ask a favor."

"What?"

"When we get to headquarters, I want permission to question at least one of the prisoners. In your presence, of course."

"Another hunch?" he asked gently.

"Not quite," I said. "But I suppose it would be, officially. It involves things that I can clear up quickly—if I'm lucky. It would take any official group quite a bit longer, and by then it would be too late."

"It's highly irregular," he said. "But I'll go along with you—until I think you're getting out of hand. If I do, I'll stop the cooperation."

"That's fair enough."

"First, though, you'll have to see the police surgeon when we get to the station. After that, you can talk to the prisoners." He sighed heavily. "And this time, try not to make a bloody mess, will you, old boy?"

We soon arrived at headquarters, where he took me in to the police surgeon. I got the full treatment on my shoulder, which hurt more than the knife had, including putting the arm in a sling, and the advice to go home and go to bed. I promised that I would, but I didn't say when I'd do it.

"All right," the Inspector said when we were in his office. "Who do you want to talk to?"

"I think Frank Burney," I said.

He nodded and picked up the phone and gave the order. About five minutes later a constable brought Burney into the office. He had one arm in a sling, too. It made me feel better.

"Sit down, Burney," the Inspector said. "Mr. March here wants to ask you some questions, and I have given him permission."

Burney sat in a chair and stared sullenly at me.

"Frank," I said, "who gave you your orders in the gang?"

"I'm not saying anything without legal advice," he said. "You don't have any proof of a gang or anything else, except a fight. So I'm not talking."

"Then I'll talk for a minute," I said cheerfully. "I think you were jobbed, Frank." He looked startled, but I went on. "I think your gang was headed by someone you never knew about. I think that you and the others got only a small percentage of what was stolen. And I think the person who was the head of the ring finally decided that it was getting too hot, and that all of you were to be thrown to the wolves. And that's what has happened, isn't it? You are here. And I'm saying that there is someone else who isn't here, and won't be unless you answer my questions."

"If what you say is right," he said, "how can I tell you the name of somebody I don't even know about?"

"I'm not asking you that," I said. "I'm asking you other things. I'm not familiar with the situation here, but I imagine that if you do cooperate and it results in the arrest of the other person, it will be to your benefit when you go into court." I looked at the Inspector.

"It would be noted," he said. "Usually the magistrates take recognition of such services to the Crown."

"I asked you who gave you your orders," I said to Burney. "Let me make a guess. It was Ma Tsing, wasn't it? He's already dead, so you can't hurt him any."

Burney hesitated a moment, then nodded. "He gave all the orders. So far as I knew, he was the head of everything."

"Good," I said. "Understand also, Frank, that I'm not trying to get you to give any information against yourself. I do consider that you have certain knowledge about this ring, but possession of knowledge about it is no confession to being involved. I also possess knowledge about what went on. Now, when jewelry was stolen, was it turned over to Ma Tsing to sell?"

"Yes."

"Ma Tsing presumably took care of selling it and then paid off everybody who had taken part?"

"Yes."

"Did you know that some of the things stolen were never sold at all?"

He looked surprised. "No. Is that true?"

"Almost eighty percent of everything that was stolen was never sold. It has vanished completely. Everything that was not sold was jade. Not only is that true, but on many jobs, other jewelry and even cash were passed up when the jade was taken."

"But everyone was paid off their share for every job," he said. He sounded bewildered.

"I know," I said. "I'm just as puzzled by it as you are. But that's the way it operated. Somebody had enough money to keep pouring it into the project. Of course, there can't be any loss. Everyone was probably paid off at fences' prices, and the jade that wasn't sold must be worth about seven or eight times that much."

He swore under his breath. "I don't get it."

"Did everybody take orders from Ma Tsing?"

"Yes."

"Tell me something else, Frank. Did Linda McKay ever have any idea that you were mixed up in something shady?"

"No."

"You got along with her? You liked her?"

"Yes."

"How come you agreed to having her kidnapped along with Mei Hsu as bait for me?"

"Ma Tsing ordered it."

"When did you and Linda become partners?"

"About five years ago."

"How did it happen?"

"She came in one day," he said, frowning. "She had papers proving she'd worked for some agency in Chicago, and she wanted to know if I was interested in selling a half interest in the agency. I needed money at the time, so we made a deal."

"It worked out pretty well?"

"Yeah. The agency made more money after she came in than it did before."

"Was that before or after you met Ma Tsing?" I asked.

"Before. Maybe six months before."

"Okay, Frank. Thanks."

The Inspector nodded to the constable, and he led Burney from the room.

"You didn't get much," Hemming said.

"I didn't need much," I said. "You feel like taking a ride?"

"All right," he said.

We went out to the police car and got in. I told the driver where to go, and we rode all the way without talking. He parked in front of the building.

"What now?" Hemming asked.

"You'd better come up with me," I said. "If I'm wrong, I may need your protection; and if I'm right, I'll need it twice as much."

We went into the building and up to her floor. I rang the bell beside the door. Hemming stood off to one side, where he wouldn't be seen right away.

She opened the door. She was wearing a dressing gown that was almost transparent. She had obviously recovered from the shock of her terrible experience. She looked as beautiful as hell—which was how beautiful she was.

"Milo," she said in surprise.

"Hello, Linda," I said. "May I come in?"

"Of course," she said, stepping back.

I went in, followed by the Inspector. Her expression changed when she saw him. She wasn't so beautiful anymore.

"What's this?" she demanded.

"This," I said, "is Inspector Hemming. You met him this afternoon."

Her gaze went from him back to me. "What the hell is this?"

"Watch her," I said to Hemming. I walked over to the miniature bookcase full of Oriental figures and studied it for a while, walking from one end to the other. Finally I found what I was looking for. At one end there was a tiny keyhole, almost completely camouflaged. I took a pick from my pocket and went to work on it

"No," she said. "You can't do that. It's private property, it's against the law. Inspector, stop him. That's burglary."

"It looks to me as if he is only examining the wood," the Inspector said carefully. "I don't see anything else."

"No!" she screamed. But after that she was quiet.

The lock gave up after about five minutes of hard work. I heard it click, and I pulled on the case that had been built against the wall. It came with my hand and the entire case swung away on well-oiled hinges.

It was a beautiful sight. What had been the original wall was covered with black velvet, and on it the jade was displayed. There was white jade, green jade, brown jade—every color and variety you could imagine. There were urns and vases, necklaces and bracelets, finger rings and thumb rings, figures and plain pieces. The wall was literally covered with jade.

"There you are, Inspector," I said. I pulled the letter from my pocket and extended it. "Here is a list of all the stolen jade insured by companies I represent. I'm sure you'll find other pieces there, but I'd like to have a receipt for these. Then, when you no longer need them for evidence, we'll recover them. I'll watch her while you check."

He took the letter and went to the wall. Linda McKay was still standing where she had been when I went to work on the lock, her gaze riveted on the wall. She was breathing rapidly, as though she'd just been running. But then suddenly her gaze shifted to me.

"You wanted to make love to me," she said.

"No longer, Linda," I said.

Her gaze darted around the room and finally came to rest on something. I looked around. It was a purse on an end table beside the couch. Just then she made a dive for it. I hit her and she collapsed on the couch. She was out. I went over and picked up the purse. There was a gun in it.

Later, with the jade packed in two of Linda's suitcases, the three of us went downstairs. I put the suitcases in the back of the police car. Then I looked at Hemming.

"Can you take her back without any help?" I asked.

"I think so," he said evenly. "I've taken in a few in my time."

"You'll be working late tonight?"

"Looks like it."

"I'll call you later," I said, "to say good-bye." I turned and walked away. A block from the apartment house, I hailed a taxi and told him to take me to the hotel.

It was just before seven when I got there. I still hadn't had any dinner, but I didn't feel hungry. I debated with myself whether I should make a phone call or pay a personal visit. Finally, I got out of the Jaguar and drove up into the hills to

Po Hing's house. After a short delay I was shown into that same room where I'd been twice before. Po Hing sat in his usual chair.

"Hiya, chum," he said. "What happened to the arm?"

"Somebody used it for target practice," I said. "Sorry to barge in like this, but I wanted to talk to you and I wasn't sure that the phone would be safe."

"Smart," he said. "Hey, why didn't you tell me that there would be cops following you around? I almost got in a jam this afternoon."

"I didn't know that there would be cops following me," I said. "As a matter of fact, there was a time when it seemed as if half of Hong Kong must have followed me. I thought that was you outside. It happened that you couldn't have timed it better. Thanks."

"Anytime," he said with a wave of his hand.

"The police got the license number of the car."

"It's okay. They'll never find it. How'd it go?"

"That bunch, plus Blake, is all under arrest. Tell me something, Hing. You thought that Blake and West were working in narcotics. Is there still a lot of it going through Hong Kong?"

"That's what I hear."

"Who's doing it?"

He shook his head. "I don't know."

"What about your own business?" I asked. "How's it doing?"

"Fine," he said. Then he looked at me. "That's not exactly the truth, pal. The last two years somebody has been beating me on a lot of jobs. And I don't know who it is. Don't that beat hell? Usually I can find out anything in this town, but now I can't even find out who's beating me at my own racket A couple of times I thought I had the guys and I took care of them, but it kept on going."

"I thought that must be so," I said. "I think it will go back to normal for you."

"Like that, huh?" he said. "Thanks, pal."

"Anytime," I said, and he grinned.

I had one short drink with him and left. I drove back to the hotel and went up to my room. It was eight o'clock. I had room service send up a double martini and some dinner and a late paper. I made myself as comfortable as I could, and waited for them to deliver. Suddenly I felt tired and lonely.

The dinner came. I signed the check and drank the martini slowly while I looked at the paper. There was no news worth reading, and the martini didn't taste good. I ate part of the dinner, but I couldn't finish it. I pushed the table away from me.

I still had to pay my bill to Jimmy, and that was all before I went back to New York. I had an idea he'd come around to collect. He knew I was leaving. So I picked up the paper and read while I waited.

Finally, there was a knock on the door. I yelled for him to come in. It was Jimmy, the usual broad smile on his face. "How are you feeling?" he asked.

"Pretty good," I said. "My shoulder is throbbing a little, but that's all. It could have been worse if you hadn't come along. I owe you a lot, Jimmy."

"I only did what was good for business," he said. "Anything else happen?"

"Not much," I said. "The police arrested Linda McKay."

"Oh?" he said. He sat down in the chair facing me. "I thought she was in the clear."

"They also recovered all of the missing jade from her apartment."

"That is a surprise," he said. He folded his arms and leaned back in the chair. "How'd they stumble on that?"

"They didn't stumble. I led them to it. I finally figured out the whole thing. It took me long enough."

"There is more?" he asked lightly.

"Much more," I said. "Jimmy, you saved my life three times and I'm grateful. I can't save your life three times, but I can save it once."

"How?"

I took the gun from the sling around my arm and pointed it at him. "By warning you in advance not to use that gun inside your coat which your fingers are touching."

"You're joking," he said, but he took his hands away from his coat.

"I'm not joking, Jimmy. Stand up." He obeyed me. "Now very carefully take off your coat and let it drop to the floor." He did, his eyes no longer friendly. I'd been right. He was wearing a shoulder holster with a gun in it.

"Now," I said, "unbuckle the holster and let it drop. But be sure your hands never get near the gun, because I'll shoot the minute they do."

He watched me the way a wild animal watches a hunter, but he did what I told him to. The gun and holster dropped with a thud.

"Kick the gun away from you," I ordered.

He did that, and it skidded several feet across the carpet. "Now, sit down again."

He obeyed. "What's this all about?" he asked.

"You know," I told him. "It's about you and Linda McKay and over two million dollars' worth of jade. You weren't kidding when you told me that you had a few other jobs. Let's see: narcotics, waterfront piracy, international jewel robbery, and the largest collection of jade around. What else?"

"You're doing the talking."

"I can't fill in all the details," I said, "but I can hit the high spots. I don't understand about you and the jade. Or Linda and the jade. I saw her face when we found it. Of course, for you, it might be like money in the bank."

"Jade is a good investment," he said.

"The way I figure it," I said, "you were an ambitious lad. You had a few things going for you, and you were making a buck. Then you got this jade bug and worked out a pretty good plan. You knew it wouldn't be good forever and someday the police would catch up with you. So you decided to stay out of sight as much as possible. Maybe you run your other rackets that way, too. Anyway, you trusted only two people: Ma Tsing, who had probably worked the narcotics racket with you, and Linda McKay, who was probably your mistress.

"Working through Ma Tsing, you got a group together: a few more Chinese, two American gunmen, and Frank Burney. Frank was valuable in a lot of ways. He also always needed money, I gather. Once you had decided on him, you sent Linda around with money to buy a half interest in his agency.

I suspect that even Ma Tsing didn't know about her. That way, she could keep an eye on things for you. It was neat. Nobody else even knew you existed.

"Then we come to Mary Moy and the jade necklace in New York. You know, in the beginning I made too much out of Mary Moy. But I finally hit on the answer about that, too. I called Pan American tonight. The flight that Mary Moy was supposed to have made didn't have a Mary Moy on it. We knew that. We'd checked it very carefully. But it did have a Mary Shan on it. A wife or a sister?"

He smiled faintly. "I am not married."

"Well, we come to my case. I got on it and by accident found a lead to Hong Kong. You had anticipated that too, but when Whitey failed, you knew that things might become risky. You decided to go out of business. And this was where you really got clever. I give you credit for that.

"On the one hand you passed orders along through Ma Tsing to have me killed, and on the other you got a job with me and made sure that you saved my life. This made you a hero to me, and prepared for the big scene in which you'd save my life again—and kill Ma Tsing at the same time. That way there was no one, except your woman, who could put the finger on you. To all intents and purposes, the gang of international thieves would all be arrested and sent away. None of them knew about you, so you and Linda would pack your little suitcases with jade and go away. It was such a pretty plot, I almost hate to spoil it."

"Why spoil it?" he asked. "There's enough for everybody."

"Not for me," I said.

"What made you think of me?" he asked.

"I didn't, until almost too late. Then it was mostly because you were always around. And when I started thinking about you, everything fell into place. Even the fact that nobody, not even Po Hing, seemed to know you; yet if you'd been the kind of operator you told me you were, everybody would have known you. And everything was a little too smooth, especially the rescues. The other night at Kai Shing's was like a beautifully staged play. It was too good—everything in its place and all with perfect timing."

"I thought it was rather well done," he said with a smile. "And Linda? You suspected her?"

"Not at first either, but she made one slip that I remembered later. In talking about the Kai Shing attempt, she wanted to know how I lost the men. Even Frank didn't know then that I had lost them; he only knew I had escaped from the club. This started me to thinking about her. She was always ready and willing to go out with me or even wait for a late call from me. Yet she didn't want to play any sort of games, romantic or otherwise. But it made sense, when I thought of her in the other way."

"You were right about Linda," he said. "She thought the jade was for her. I considered it an investment for me. But I have other investments. Are you sure you wouldn't like to share them with me?"

"Quite sure," I said. "Money goes to my head. I joined Riches Anonymous a long time ago."

I used my left hand to pick up the phone. It hurt like hell, but I managed it. I called Inspector Hemming and told him to come over because I had another customer for him. He said he'd be right there. I replaced the phone and looked at Jimmy. He was smiling broadly again.

"You seem pretty cheerful for a guy who's going to jail," I said.

"I was just thinking how much you've upset the Inspector's routine," he said. "As for me, the picture is much less serious than you think. There is no one who can testify against me except Linda. I doubt if she will, but even if she does, I don't think I will be convicted by that. Would such a clever man give all that jade to his girl? And they won't be able to locate Mary Shan. You have done an admirable job of reconstructing what happened, but fortunately, none of it is provable without witnesses."

Inspector Hemming made it in twenty minutes. He came in, and I gave him the story briefly. Hemming put some cuffs on Jimmy and started to lead him away.

"You'll be down tomorrow to make a complete statement before you leave?" he asked.

"Yes," I said.

"You are leaving tomorrow?" he said.

"Yes."

"Good. I really appreciate what you've done in this case, but I do think it would be better for everyone if you left within the next twenty-four hours." Then he was gone with his prisoner.

I put my gun away and got the jade figure from the dresser drawer. I went downstairs, stopping at the desk long enough to send a cablegram to Robert Carlin. It read:

EVERYTHING RECOVERED. LEAVING HONG KONG TOMORROW.

MILO

Then I went on to Mei's apartment. She was waiting for me with a glass of Lor Mai Tsao and open arms.

The next morning Mei went with me to my hotel. I got my things and checked out, and we went to police headquarters. I dictated a long statement and signed it. Then we drove the Jaguar to the ferry landing. Mei would return it to the garage on her way home. And she'd take the jade back to her father.

We rode the ferry over to Kowloon, and I checked my baggage on the plane and confirmed my reservation. There were a few minutes before flight time, so we wandered around the terminal, not saying much. There wasn't much we could say.

Finally, it was time to board the plane. We were passing a vending machine with lichee nuts. I put in a coin and got a handful. I gave them to Mei.

"I wish they were diamonds, darling," I said. "Diamonds for a real lady, instead of jade for one that wasn't."

"I will string them and wear them anyway," she said softly.

I kissed her and got on the plane quickly. It took off and we were soon climbing over the crouching hills which were known as the Nine Dragons. The blue sea was flecked with gold.

ABOUT THE AUTHOR

Kendell Foster Crossen
(1910–1981), the only child
of Samuel Richard Cros-
sen and Clo Foster Cros-
sen, was born on a farm
outside Albany in Athens
County, Ohio—a village of
some 550 souls in the year
of this birth. His ancestors
on his mother's side include
the 19th-century songwriter
Stephen Collins Foster
("Oh! Susanna"); William
Allen, founder of Allentown, Pennsylvania; and Ebenezer
Foster, one of the Minute Men who sprang to arms at the
Lexington alarm in April 1775.

Ken went to Rio Grande College on a football scholarship
but stayed only one year. "When I was fairly young, I devel-
oped the disgusting habit of reading," says Milo March,
and it seems Ken Crossen, too, preferred self-education.
He loved literature and poetry; favorite authors included
Christopher Marlowe and Robert Service. He also enjoyed
participant sports and was a semi-pro fighter in the heavy-

weight class. He became a practicing magician and had a passion for chess.

After college Ken wrote several one-act plays that were produced in a small Cleveland theater. He worked in steel mills and Fisher Body plants. Then he was employed as an insurance investigator, or "claims adjuster," in Cleveland. But he left the job and returned to the theater, now as a performer: a tumbling clown in the Tom Mix Circus; a comic and carnival barker for a tent show, and an actor in a medicine show.

In 1935, Ken hitchhiked to New York City with a typewriter under his arm, and found work with the WPA Writers' Project, covering cricket for the *New York City Guidebook*. In 1936, he was hired by the Munsey Publishing Company as associate editor of the popular *Detective Fiction Weekly*. The company asked him to come up with a character to compete with The Shadow, and thus was born a unique superhero of pulps, comic books, and radio—The Green Lama, an American mystic trained in Tibetan Buddhism.

Crossen sold his first story, "The Aaron Burr Murder Case," to *Detective Fiction Weekly* in September 1939, but says he didn't begin to make a living from writing till 1941. He tried his hand at publishing true crime magazines, comics, and a picture magazine, without great success, so he set out for Hollywood. From his typewriter flowed hundreds of stories, short novels for magazines, scripts radio, television, and film, nonfiction articles. He delved into science fiction in the 1950s, starting with "Restricted Clientele" (February 1951). His dystopian novels *Year of Consent* and *The Rest Must Die* also appeared in this decade.

In the course of his career Ken Crossen acquired six pseud-onyms: Richard Foster, Bennett Barlay, Kent Richards, Clay Richards, Christopher Monig, and M.E. Chaber. The variety was necessary because different publishers wanted to reserve specific bylines for their own publications. Ken based "M.E. Chaber" on the Hebrew word for "author," *mechaber*.

In the early '50s, as M.E. Chaber, Crossen began to write a series of full-length mystery/espionage novels featuring Milo March, an insurance investigator. The first, *Hangman's Harvest*, was published in 1952. In all, there are twenty-two Milo March novels. One, *The Man Inside*, was made into a British film starring Jack Palance.

Most of Ken's characters were private detectives, and Milo was the most popular. Paperback Library reissued twenty-five Crossen titles in 1970–1971, with covers by Robert McGin-nis. Twenty were Milo March novels, four featured an insur-ance investigator named Brian Brett, and one was about CIA agent Kim Locke.

Crossen excelled at producing well-plotted entertainment with fast-moving action. His research skills were a strong asset, back when research meant long hours searching library microfilms and poring over street maps and hotel floorplans. His imagination took him to many international hot spots, although he himself never traveled abroad. Like Milo March, he hated flying ("When you've seen one cloud, you've seen them all").

Ken Crossen was married four times. With his first wife he had three children (Stephen, Karen, Kendra) and with his second a son (David). He lived in New York, Florida, Southern California, Nevada, and other parts of the country. Milo March moves from Denver to New York City after five books of the series, with an apartment on Perry Street in Greenwich Village; that's where Ken lived, too. His and Milo's favorite watering hole was the Blue Mill Tavern, a short walk from the apartment.

Ken Crossen was a combination of many of the traits of his different male characters: tough, adventuresome, with a taste for gin and shapely women. But perhaps the best observation was made in an obituary written by sci-fi writer Avram Davidson, who described Ken as a fundamentally gentle person who had been buffeted by many winds.